Crows Creek

The nephew of President Hayes has been murdered in Crows Creek, so he orders the governor to hire a first class marshal, someone with a proven track record for solving crimes. Unfortunately, the best person for the job is Daniel Wheetman, an Englishman who has no experience of the West; he cannot ride or shoot, and his abrupt manner and lack of social skills would only mean a quick and violent death. So a rough tough cowboy called Murphy is hired to keep the marshal alive.

Daniel is under the misconception that all villains will automatically surrender once challenged by an officer of the law, whereas Murphy has a 'shoot now, ask questions later' policy. Together they take on a powerful cattle baron and a corrupt sheriff.

Crows Creek

John E. Vale

A Black Horse Western

ROBERT HALE

© John E. Vale 2018
First published in Great Britain 2018

ISBN 978-0-7198-2783-9

The Crowood Press
The Stable Block
Crowood Lane
Ramsbury
Marlborough
Wiltshire SN8 2HR

www.bhwesterns.com

Robert Hale is an imprint
of The Crowood Press

Typeset by
Derek Doyle & Associates, Shaw Heath
Printed and bound in Great Britain by
4Bind Ltd, Stevenage, SG1 2XT

CHAPTER 1

'John Murphy Samuel Patterson, also known as Texas Pat, Sam Murphy, and John Patterson, you have been found guilty of the charges brought against you. Namely, three charges of bank robbery, two cases of horse thieving, bigamy, rustling cattle and cheating at cards.' The judge looked solemnly at Murphy, shook his head and gave a sigh. 'Have you anything to say in your defence before I pronounce sentence?'

Murphy rose to his full height of six foot four and clasped his massive, handcuffed hands on the bar in front of him. It was the culmination of a two-day trial, during which Murphy vehemently, and with great energy, denied every charge several times and cursed at every juncture. By some miracle he'd managed to avoid being charged with contempt of court for blaspheming in the most outrageous fashion and trying to assault every witness, whether hostile or not, but finally, with everything taken into account, he accepted the verdict for what it was: a complete miscarriage of justice!

5

Slowly and deliberately, he surveyed the faces of everyone present, staring deep with his dark brown eyes and keeping his iron jaw shut tightly. His leathered face began to change shape as a kindly smile appeared and he began to loosen his weathered lips. 'I ain't never cheated at cards,' he said, as his smile grew wider.

The judge picked up his gavel and was about to speak, but Murphy held up his hand to pronounce silence. 'Wait! There's somethin' I wanna say.'

'Go ahead, and be brief,' the judge replied.

'Those charges are all a pile of trumped up bullshit,' he shouted as he leered at the jury. He pointed to the man at the far left. 'That's Jacob Wilcox and he owes me thirty-five dollars for the work I did repairing his fences. He'd sell his own Grandmother for thirty-five dollars.'

The shocked crowd began to mutter as the judge banged his gavel. 'Order! Order!' he shouted.

With little fear of consequence, Murphy pointed to a fat man sitting at the back and continued. 'I bought those horses in good faith from the brother of that barrel of lard sat there and he knows it.'

'Order! I call this court to order!'

Two clerks standing either side of Murphy calmed him down and he slumped back into his chair.

The judge gave him a withering look and pointed at Murphy with his gavel. 'You, sir, are very fortunate not to be found in contempt of court for that little outburst, but I am a tolerant man and realise the strain you must be under,' he straightened his tie and

6

gave a cough. 'Now, it is the order of this court for you to go to prison for a period of five years, during which time you will serve hard labour until you manage to see the error of your ways.'

Murphy exploded to his feet. 'Five years?' he screamed. 'Why, you son of a bitch, you can just take those five years and shove 'em up your backside.'

Crashing his gavel down in anger, the judge shouted. 'Now you ARE in contempt! Eight years!'

'Why, you slimy polecat, you can't do that,' Murphy screamed. 'You're the son of a cathouse whore. If I ever get my hands on you, I'll rip your scrawny little head off.'

'Twelve years.'

'Twelve years? You bald-headed, ass-licking, mule-brained varmint.'

'Let's make it an even twenty,' the judge smirked.

Murphy's face went red with rage as he was man-handled out of the dock. With the strength of five men, he began bucking and bending and managed to throw the usher clinging to his left-hand-side halfway across the room easily and, with a sharp lift of one elbow, the other fell backwards to the floor. Apart from the minor handicap of wearing handcuffs he was free and, like a cougar, Murphy sprung over chairs, benches and balustrades and slammed against the rostrum as he desperately lunged towards the judge's throat, but the rostrum was too high and Murphy fell back to the floor where several men pinned him down.

Still screaming with rage, a sympathetic voice hit

his ears and calmed the savage beast inside him. 'John! Listen to me, it's Leroy.'

Like a train letting off steam, Murphy's body quickly deflated. 'Leroy? Is that you?'

'I was at the back. I didn't want you to see me. Besides, if Ma would have found out I didn't get you out of this mess, she'd have taken a switch to my backside like she used to when we were kids.'

Murphy rolled to the side and began to laugh uncontrollably. 'Oh, shucks. Now I'll come quietly. Just let me have a word with my baby brother.' He stood up and grabbed his brother's head fondly, giving a deep smile that penetrated Leroy's heart. 'How is Ma?'

'Since Pa passed away, she's never been the same. She spends most of her time sittin' next to his grave, tellin' him about the farm and how you're goin' to come home one day with a blushin' bride to help her with all the chores. She tells him how well you're doin' and how you write now and then. She reads him your letters time and time again. I swear if I hadn't written 'em myself I'd believe 'em.'

A tear welled up in the giant man's eye. 'You go and tell Ma that's the way it is. Don't tell her – well, you know, don't tell her the truth.'

Leroy dropped his gaze to the floor. 'I reckon it'd kill her, bro.'

Murphy let go sadly and walked towards the court-room door slowly. 'I reckon you're right,' he whispered. 'I reckon you're right.'

'John!' Leroy shouted, as he raised his right hand

8

gently. 'God bless.'

Murphy stopped in the doorway, turned and grinned. 'God?' he gave a tut. 'He's got a lot of explaining to do when we get eye to eye.'

Leroy watched as Murphy disappeared out of sight.

'My, my.' His trance was broken by a squeaky little voice. 'You were right, Clarence; that is the man we're looking for.'

'I thought you would agree when you saw him, Claude.'

Leroy turned to see two identical twins clutching briefcases under their right arms. They wore dark suits covering starched white shirts, dazzlingly split with bright red ties. Slightly overweight, they stood just over five feet tall and their balding heads gave them a piggy look. 'Well, well,' Claude said. 'We must have a word with the judge straight away.'

'You take to words right out of my mouth,' Clarence replied. 'Right out of my mouth.'

'Quick,' Claude said.

'Yes, we must be quick.'

Together they entered the judge's chambers and stood proudly in front of him.

The judge looked up, slightly confused. 'Who may you two be?'

Clarence moved silently towards him, passed a calling card and reversed back. Claude did the same. 'We,' Clarence began. 'We, that is, the two of us, are empowered by the governor to make a certain deal.'

'Oh yes,' Claude confirmed. 'A certain deal – yes indeed.'

'We need to employ Mr Patterson,' Clarence began. 'The governor has empowered us to make a deal.'

'Ah,' Claude interrupted. 'We've already informed His Honour of that, my dear brother.'

'Quite so,' he agreed. 'Quite so. You see, Mr Patterson has certain talents we would like to avail ourselves of and feel it may be beneficial for all parties to make a certain deal.' Both twins reached into their briefcases. Each took out a single sheet of paper and placed them on the judge's desk.

Claude gave a little cough. 'This is a free pardon for whomsoever. All we have to do is fill in the relevant details and you have to sign it.'

The judge stared in total disbelief. 'Are you two completely out of your minds?'

'Not us, you understand,' Clarence pointed out. 'It's the governor who has instructed us and thus you are intimating the governor is out of his mind.'

'Oh dear,' Claude said. 'That would never do.'

'No indeed, not at all.'

'He can't do this,' the judge insisted.

Claude pointed to the documents. 'They also have the signature of the president himself, Rutherford B. Hayes.'

The judge rubbed his furrowed brow. 'You mean to tell me . . .'

'We have just told you.'

'Oh yes, we have indeed. Hmmm, yes.'

'Now, Your Honour, perhaps you'll be quite so kind as to tell us where we may find Mr Patterson?'

10

'Well, I guess he'll be in the prison wagon, possibly on his way.'

'Oh dear, that will never do,' Claude mumbled.

'Clerk! Clerk!' the judge shouted. 'Where is that fellow when you need him?'

The door burst open. 'Your Honour?' said a thin man whilst rubbing his arm in pain.

Clarence was quick to speak. 'Be so kind as to stop Mr Patterson and ask him if he wouldn't mind coming back and having a word with us.'

'Sir?' he gasped.

'You heard,' the judge pointed out in defeat.

'Yes, sir, right away.'

The three waited in complete silence until the door opened once again. In its frame stood Murphy, still in handcuffs but now wearing shackles on his legs as an extra precaution. He stood like stone.

'Please, Mr Patterson,' Claude began. 'Please take a seat. We have a certain deal to put your way.'

Murphy did not move.

Clarence took a chair and dragged it close to Murphy. 'Please take a seat, Mr Patterson.'

Murphy sat down slowly. 'What the cotton pickin' is goin' on now?'

Claude began. 'Well, as I said to His Honour, we have a certain deal that you may be interested in.'

Murphy's eyes moved between one twin and the other. 'Go on.'

'We,' Clarence said. 'That is, myself, my brother, His Honour, the governor and the president of the USA himself have a certain deal to put your way.'

'Go on.'

'Well, in return for certain services you may well find yourself with a free pardon.'

'No, dear brother,' Clarence interrupted. 'He *will* find himself with a full pardon.'

'Of course, dear brother. You *will* find yourself with a full pardon.'

Murphy, who wore a handsome droopy moustache, rubbed his smooth-shaven chin. 'What exactly do I have to do?'

'Oh, that's the easy part,' Clarence giggled. 'You become the sworn deputy of a certain Marshal Wheetman, or should I say *to* Marshal Wheetman, or is it *for*?'

Seconds passed that seemed like an eternity to Murphy. 'A deputy?' he gasped. 'What sort of deputy?'

'Oh, just the regular kind,' Claude explained.

Clarence clapped his hands in excited delight. 'Oh, tell him, tell him the rest.'

'Oh yes, of course I will.' He took a deep breath. 'Mr Patterson, you will work as a deputy for two years, and after such time receive a bonus of twenty thousand dollars. In the meantime you will receive a regular wage, which can be drawn from any bank you choose, subject to us having made certain arrangements in advance.'

'Well, I don't rightly know. . . . What about old Sea Biscuit?'

'The strawberry roan? We have checked its whereabouts and as far as we are aware it is in the livery stable. That being the case, you get your horse and saddle back with all bills having been paid.'

'My guns?'

'Those as well.'

'All of 'em?'

'Yes,' Claude replied, as Clarence handed him an inventory. 'Looking at this list, your belongings amount to one loaded yellowboy rifle with a star brand on the stock; one Colt .45 handgun containing five bullets, plus holster containing a further eight bullets; a Colt pocket revolver, fully loaded; a broken silver pocket watch with brown leather lanyard; and a cream Stetson hat trimmed with tin badges.'

'That's a downright lie: they're solid silver,' Murphy interrupted.

'Oh dear, Mr Patterson, you will have to take that up with your hatter.' He looked at Murphy and smiled. 'Three dollars and fifty-nine cents; five cheroots; some loose tobacco; a deck of marked cards; plus a lady's garter with the name Belle embroidered upon it.'

'Well done, Claude. I do like the bit about the lady's garter. Anyway, Mr Patterson, you will receive all your belongings back, for what they are worth, and the prison sentence will be suspended for two years, starting today.'

Murphy shook his head. 'There has to be a catch.'

'No catch,' Claude replied. 'Just a simple clause, which is to say, should Marshal Wheetman meet his demise before the end of the contract period, the whole deal will be considered null and void and you will be required to surrender yourself for incarceration for the said period of twenty years.'

'Let's get this straight,' Murphy began. 'All I have to do is keep this marshal alive for two years and I'm a free man with twenty thousand dollars?'

'Correct,' they both said.

'He's a well man, not ailin' at all?'

'A very well man, we are given to believe.'

He beamed with delight. 'Where do I sign?'

Within minutes, the initial paperwork was done, and Murphy was freed from his shackles. As he rubbed his wrists a thought came to mind. 'Errr . . . one little thing.'

'Yes?' they said.

'What if he dies from smallpox?'

'You lose.'

'Cholera?'

'You lose.'

'Quicksand?'

'You lose.'

'Snake bite?'

'You lose.'

Murphy looked into the air, smiled, walked up to the judge's desk, opened a box, took out a cigar and took a satisfying draw as he lit it. 'Ah, what am I worrying about? He's a real marshal, right? What could go wrong?'

CHAPTER 2

Murphy's first glance at the town of Crows Creek was from a seat of the Lincoln Flier as it pulled into the station slowly. It looked much like any other town of its kind; a ramshackle collection of random buildings disjointed in every way.

Murphy had spent all his adult years as a cowboy or on the run as an outlaw, and was tired of having to sleep whenever it was possible, eating from the back of a chuckwagon or surviving on hardtack and beans, so the chance to travel in comfort on the Lincoln Flier was much too difficult to pass up.

As the train panted patiently in the station, belching steam and puffing smoke, porters and passengers hurried here and there like ants over warm cotton candy. Murphy strolled quietly and with purpose to the livery car just behind the caboose, swung the locking lever over, slid the door open and went inside. To the far left he could see Sea Biscuit, saddled and tethered just as he had left her. She gave a slight whinny, threw her head up and down and stamped her feet when she set eyes on him. The two had been together for eight years and she almost knew him better than he did himself. There was an instance in Dodge when a rather drunken Murphy had been caught in the arms of another man's wife. As Murphy staggered, ran and rolled down the main street, trying his best to put his pants back on, the irate husband filled his scattergun with two cartridges full of rock salt with the sole intent of destroying any marital prospects Murphy may have been fostering. The faithful Sea Biscuit galloped to the rescue and bowled the man over with a shoulder charge. Murphy was far too drunk to function and, with his pants still around his ankles, Sea Biscuit galloped away with Murphy clinging to her saddle and rattling around like a rag doll.

There was also the time when Sheriff Doogan, who was riding at the head of a six-man posse, put a bullet into Murphy's right leg. He would have bled to death had Sea Biscuit not realised the situation and managed to outrun his pursuers before taking him to Doc Wallace. Doc Wallace took the view that a man in need, no matter who or why, would be treated with discretion and respect with no questions asked.

And there's the famous, rather dubious story about when Murphy was down to his last dollar: she even took him to the Last Drop Saloon and stamped twelve times with her front foot. Quick as a flash, Murphy went to the wheel, dropped his last dollar on red number twelve and won twenty-five dollars. Now, it may have been revenge; who knows? But because he left Sea Biscuit tethered up outside the saloon whilst he spent fifteen of the twenty-five dollars on whiskey and a cathouse floozy called Mavis, Sea Biscuit gave him seven more tips, all of which proved worthless.

Murphy gave her a few pats as he dropped his hexagonal barrelled yellowboy carbine into her saddle holster, then led her out into the brightness of the day and tied her to the black iron station railings that ran from one end of the platform to the other. 'Hey, mister.' A voice came from behind. 'You can't leave that thing there; we've got a railway to run.' At that precise moment, Sea Biscuit decided to put forward her point of view. 'Woah!' the man screamed. 'What do you call that?'

Without a word, Murphy strolled back for his saddlebags, picked them up, returned slowly and threw them over Sea Biscuit's back. 'Where in the name of hell have you been, my friend? Do you mean to say you don't recognize horse shit when you see it?'

The man pointed his finger and gave it a waggle. 'I'll . . . I'll . . . I'll . . . You'll see I don't!'

Murphy tightened Sea Biscuit's girth strap, took the pummel in his massive hand, placed his left foot in the stirrup and swung into the saddle as if that's where he belonged forever. 'Tell you what, my friend, let me give you a tip: put your finger in it whilst it's still warm, taste it, and if it tastes like horse shit then for God's sake don't tread in it.'

The man could hear Murphy's laughter for a full

five minutes after he'd ridden away towards Crows Creek.

Following the brief instructions given to him after the trial, Murphy stopped outside the Star Diamond Hotel. The day was still quite young so he tied Sea Biscuit to the horse rail, slid his yellowboy out and hammered on the locked doors. After a moment, two bolts could be heard sliding away and one door opened.

'Murphy?' a red haired woman asked.

'Yep,' he replied.

She stood back and beckoned him to enter. 'Come in, you're expected,' she said.

Murphy gave his eyes chance to grow accustom to the dark indoors before easing his grip on his rifle. He didn't know what to expect until the marshal arrived the following day, but over the years he'd learned to trust no one and expect trouble to be around every corner. The place was empty with the exception of the woman, two stubby, well-dressed gentlemen wearing grey suits and pork pie hats, and a man behind the bar.

'Boys! Is that you?' Murphy asked with delight.

Clarence and Claude turned round in unison and smiled. 'It is indeed,' said one. 'Indeed,' said the other.

Murphy was glad to see the two little piggies because he was still a little confused as to what his job was exactly, or where he could get his weekly wages, and what Marshal Wheetman looked like. 'Now, which one of you two is Charley and which one is

18

Chester? You're like peas in a pod; I sure don't know which is which.'

The one on the left pointed to the other. 'He's Clarence and I'm Claude.'

'No,' the other replied. 'He's Clarence and I'm Claude.'

Murphy gave out a hearty laugh. 'Shucks, boys, you're yankin' my handle now.'

'Handle?' Claude asked.

'Well, no, what I mean to say is it sure is a surprise to see you two here.' He looked around anxiously. 'You ain't got that judge with yer, have yer?'

'No, it's just the two of us.' One of them gestured to the silver-haired man behind the counter. 'And of course Mr McKay, who is your most gracious host and, may we add, somewhat of a confidant?'

Murphy walked slowly towards the man, who was aged about forty with a craggy face below a slick head of silver hair. The man wore a white-frilled lace shirt with gold armbands and a black bowtie. Murphy held out his hand in gesture. 'They call me Murphy,' he said with confidence.

McKay grasped his hand. 'Aye, and they call me Colin, tha ken?' He gave a broad smile.

Murphy looked slightly confused. 'You're not from round these parts?' he asked.

'Glasgow in Scotland, if ye ken? Althooo 'ave been here some ten years noo.'

'You sure talk funny,' he laughed. 'I had a friend called Jimmy Campbell – came from Scotland too, but he didn't talk the way you do.'

'Agh! A Campbell, ye say? There's naer been anything so low doon despicable and snake-bellied as a Campbell, I'll tell ye that for nowt. They're nairn worth pishin' on if they were afire.'

He poured two shots of whiskey. 'Tha'll nay see a man drink on his own, Murphy?'

'Now you're speaking my language,' he replied with a large grin, before tipping a whiskey down his throat. 'Now, what's all this about? How come these two boys know you, and what do you know about Marshal Wheetman?'

Colin leaned closer over his bar. 'There's an element in this toon, a certain element that needs ta be stopped.' He poured two more whiskeys and tipped his down his throat quickly. 'Fe the good of the toon, ye ken? There's a future here for families and their wee ons, good families who want ta make hoomes here, and we're bein' chased away by Joe Bannister and his henchmen. As for the new marshal, I know nowt at all.'

Murphy turned to the twins. 'Go ahead, boys, fill us in.'

They both looked confused at one another. 'We can honestly say we have never met Mr Wheetman, but as you may be aware, he will arrive from the east on the Lincoln Flier's return journey tomorrow.'

Murphy reached into his top pocket, took out a cheroot, placed it between his lips and struck a match on the bar top. As the clouds of smoke began to gather, he grinned. 'One thing's for certain: Marshal Wheetman must be one tough son of a bitch.'

The twins both gave a cough. 'We have taken the liberty to draw up a contract, Mr Patterson, which we need you to sign as soon as you have assured us you are the man for the job.'

Murphy gasped a cloud of smoke. 'Now just a cotton pickin' moment! No one said anything about no contract. Just what in the name of hell are you two after?'

'Oh, nothing at all, except that since we have spoken with our employer he, or they, wish us to test how good you are.'

'Good?'

'Yes, good,' Claude said, 'with such things as marksmanship, so we have set up a little test round the back. Please follow us.'

The three strolled round the building until they found themselves in a sandy corral with six cans placed on top of one of the fences. 'Mr Patterson,' Clarence said, pointing to the cans. 'Would you be so kind as to shoot at those?'

'From where?' Murphy drawled.

'Right from where you stand,' Claude replied.

'And who's gonna pay for the cartridges?'

'Pay? We don't quite get what you mean; surely they can't be very expensive.'

Murphy narrowed his eyes, trapping them in a stare from hell. 'Five bits a piece and there's six cans, that makes ...' He looked to the heavens as he counted with his fingers. 'Horseshit! Whatever it comes to is more than I wanna pay.'

'We do hope you're not trying to get out of it, Mr

Patterson,' Claude said.

Murphy turned his head and rolled his cheroot to the left hand corner of his mouth. 'A dollar a can,' he demanded.

The twins looked at one another. 'Very well,' they agreed.

Murphy flipped the safety loop from over the hammer on his sidearm and lifted the Colt out casually.

'No, Mr Murphy,' they said in unison.

'What we require is to see you draw and shoot, as it were,' Clarence said. 'All in the same action, so to speak.'

Murphy looked at them, grinned and placed a sixth cartridge in the empty chamber of his Colt nonchalantly. He spun it backwards round his index finger and dropped it skilfully back into his holster. Almost immediately he drew and began rapid fire, fanning the hammer with his left hand until all six had gone.

After the smoke cleared and the sound of the last can rolling down the rocks had ceased, Clarence gave a nervous cough. 'Well, that all seems to be in order, Mr Patterson. If you would be so kind as to follow us back inside and put your mark on our agreement, we will leave you alone.'

Murphy put his large frame in their way and held out his hand. 'Six dollars,' he drawled.

'Oh my,' Clarence said as he fumbled through his pockets. 'Of course; here's three from me.'

Murphy turned his head slowly to peer menacingly

at Claude. 'Oh my, of course.' He handed him a ten-dollar note. 'Errr, this is all I have, so if you have any change. . . ?'

Murphy thought, rubbed his chin and handed Claude three dollars. 'I reckon that'll be quits.'

'Oh, but I gave you ten dollars,' Claude protested.

'And I gave you three back,' Murphy growled.

'But that was from Clarence.'

'And now it's from me. Let's go back inside. I'm real thirsty.'

As the three went back inside the hotel, Murphy saw the woman who had originally let him in standing behind the bar instead of Colin. She was tall, slim and wore a flamboyant dress cut low at the front, and her red hair cascaded over her milky-white shoulders. She looked up at Murphy and smiled. 'Another drink, Mr Patterson?' she asked, as she poured him one nonetheless. 'By the sounds of it, you boys been havin' fun.'

'Now you know who I am, pretty lady, but who might you be?' Murphy asked.

'Back off, tiger, I'm the lady of the house.' She put the cork back into the bottle and leaned knowingly at the back of the bar. 'Mrs Alice McKay, and don't you go forgettin' it.'

Murphy picked up his glass to toast. 'To friends,' he said.

'Friends indeed,' she replied.

Mrs McKay was once a saloon girl with little chance of betterment except for her good looks. As soon as Colin McKay clapped eyes on her in Reno he wanted her as his wife, so he tried to buy her. Her employer; Lloyd Strong, had taken her from her father in lieu of a hundred dollar gambling debt and wasn't going to let her go without what he called a little fun. He agreed to accept one hundred dollars, but Colin had to shoot an apple off her head in order to seal the bargain. Unfortunately, Colin had spent rather a long time at the bar before he agreed to the trial and his aim may have been compromised some-what. His first – and best – shot missed inches to the left, much to the amusement of the large crowd that had gathered in the background. His second shot shattered a wooden pineapple sitting atop the stair-case strut. After his third hit a stuffed bear, the crowd reached total hysteria. The fourth hit the wall; the fifth, a door; and the sixth disappeared without a trace.

Lloyd was laughing so much that he could hardly speak as he slapped Colin on the back. 'Take her,' he boomed. 'She's yours.'

Hearing this, Alice gritted her teeth, marched over to Lloyd and hit him directly on the nose. At first, Lloyd's eyes went wide, then to slits as he began to laugh uncontrollably once again. Alice grabbed Colin's hand and dragged him out. Soon after they were man and wife, and very happy too.

Murphy rubbed his smooth chin in deep contempla-tion. 'Then I guess you're the wife of the proprietor?'

'Colin!' she gasped. 'If Colin owned it, there

would come a day when he'd lose it in some poker game.'

'So you bought it?'

'Nope, I won it from Colin in a poker game.'

Murphy burst into belly laughter. 'Well, don't that beat all,' he coughed.

Alice looked at the twins and nodded to Murphy. 'Those two give me the creeps,' she whispered. 'I don't know which one's which and I trust 'em as much as I trust a rattler in my corset.'

'I knows just what you mean, and something tells me there's more layers to this onion than we think.'

CHAPTER 3

Murphy always woke at dawn. It was probably a habit he'd picked up when he was a trailhand or outlaw. He opened the curtains and scratched his crotch. Sweat from his groin and underarms had stained his long johns and vest, so much so that it didn't come out even after he'd taken a bath wearing them. However, despite his Spartan outlook for his personal hygiene, he always shaved his chin and neck.

Using cold water and a knife, he cringed as the blade ripped whisker after whisker until the job was done painfully, then grinned as he watched himself in the mirror, using a towel to wipe off any excess soap.

The job having been done, he went out into the early morning air and took a good deep breath. Due to his life revolving around horses, his nostrils were so accustomed to the smell of horse dung, no matter what state of freshness it was in; the large piles of it scattered here and there almost enhanced the delicious aroma drifting from the restaurant a few buildings down. *Bacon and eggs,* he thought.

As he entered the restaurant the warm smells and chink of crockery reminded him of those childhood days back on the farm when Ma would get out her best plates and saucers and entertain visitors, and he began to smile, but as he thought longer his smile turned to a grimace when he remembered the last visitor was the bank manager coming to serve an eviction notice. His pa broke his leg falling off a horse and Murphy, being the older son, tried to keep the place going, but he was only nine years old and could barely keep food on the table, so the rent fell into arrears.

The bank manager was a greedy man and quick to see a profit. Within days of the Patterson family having been thrown out, he sold it for three times what he gave them for it. With the help of Pastor Morgan and members of his congregation, the Patterson family managed to buy a smaller place, but it never paid much and Murphy was sent out to work at the livery stables. There he met Mat Wilding, a rough, tough ex soldier who taught Murphy how to use a gun, rope cattle, throw a knife and, unfortunately, cheat at cards. Wilding had lost a leg in the war so he couldn't ride as good as he used to, nor groom a horse as before, so he was glad to employ Murphy and almost looked upon him as the son he never had.

Murphy was paid for every horse he turned out, as well as tips, which were plentiful due to the attention to detail he achieved. Mat Wilding's livery business was doing very well and Murphy worked his day off to get more money, but unfortunately Mat caught the pox and died. His sister sold it to the Carpenter family, who didn't need Murphy, so at the age of fourteen Murphy began herding cattle and drifted away slowly from his family.

'I'll be with you in a minute!' came a voice that snatched him out of his thoughts. 'Just take a seat and I'll bring some hot coffee.'

His early morning gravel voice echoed from wall to wall. 'Just as you say,' he replied, as he looked for a table in a far corner. Over his thirty-five years he had learned never to sit with his back to the door, just in case the law should arrive. He didn't quite realise that he was the law this time.

Before many minutes had passed, an elderly lady wearing a dark, flour-stained pinafore came out of the back room. She was brushing herself down as she walked towards his table. 'Now, what can I get you, stranger?'

Murphy, remembering what she had shouted, removed his hat, looked up and smiled. 'Coffee?'

'Oh my, I'd forget my head if it wasn't screwed on.' Quick as a flash, she took a pot of coffee from atop the stove and poured him a cup. 'And something to eat?'

'Bacon and eggs will do just fine, ma'am.'

She nodded. 'Bacon and eggs it is then. And no fresh baked bread? I was up before dawn baking it.'

Murphy sniffed the air with delight. 'Well, ma'am,

I reckon I will, and if it tastes as good as it smells, I'll be in heaven.'

'And pancakes?'

'With syrup?'

'Why, of course.'

'Ma'am, I am in heaven.'

'I'll bring your pancakes first,' she said cheerily. 'I won't be long.'

Moments after she had gone the door burst open and two young men took seats at the table nearest to door. They were in good spirits and were almost giggling like naughty children. 'Hey, Katie,' one of them shouted, 'let's have some service.'

'Help yourself to coffee, boys. I'm just doing the gentleman some pancakes; won't be long.'

'Aw, come on, Katie, we're hungry,' insisted one. 'He won't mind if we have them.' They looked at Murphy and grinned. 'Hey! You won't mind, will you, mister?'

Ignoring them, Murphy said nothing. He lit a cheroot, took a long draw and sipped his coffee.

'Hey, mister,' one shouted. 'We're talking to you.'

Murphy looked up, stony-faced. 'You boys late for school or something?'

'Boys? Hell, mister, you don't know who you're talking to.'

'Don't reckon I do,' he replied calmly.

'We're the Bannister Boys.'

'Is that a fact? Now, why don't you two puppies go home and tell mummy you're hungry and leave a man to have his breakfast?'

'You didn't hear right, mister. I said we're the Bannister Boys.'

Murphy stood up to his full height and unclipped his Colt. 'Now I normally do my killin' after breakfast but if you *boys* insist, I'll make an exception.'

One of them looked at the other and gulped but the other stood up to show Murphy down. 'Apologize!' he said, but Murphy heard a nervous tremor in his voice.

'Don't do it son. I'll send ya to hell.'

'Leave it, Carl, he's not worth it,' said the other.

Carl's eyes went from side to side as he pointed at Murphy. 'Mister, this is your lucky day,' Carl said, backing out of the door slowly.

Murphy didn't re-clip his .45; he just sat down and drank his coffee, keeping an eye on the door.

Katie came back. 'Mister, all I can say is drink your drink, eat your meal and go. I don't want any trouble in here.'

Murphy complained like a scolded child. 'But ma'am, I didn't start anything; they did.'

'You could have let them have your pancakes.'

'But them thern pancakes is rightfully mine!'

'That's nothing to do with it,' she snapped back, holding out her hand. 'And that will be two dollars in advance if you please.'

'Two dollars! In advance?' he gasped.

'Two dollars for losing me the custom of those two boys, and I want it in advance before you get yourself killed.'

'Aw, shucks, they was just two boys letting of a bit

of steam.'

'Boys or no boys, they were the Bannister Boys, and you'll do right to remember that.'

Murphy reluctantly handed over two dollars, sucked on his teeth and shook his head. 'Ma'am, if the rest of this town is as friendly as you are I'll wager you don't get many visitors coming back.'

'That's between me and the garden post,' she replied as she walked away.

The restaurant began to fill with more customers, trailhands mostly, but one or two townsfolk mixed here and there. Murphy kept his head down and ate his breakfast slowly. After he'd finished he made his way outside and slapped his stomach with pleasure.

Whilst in the restaurant, Murphy hadn't noticed the town had become alive, with people rushing around. Wagons rattled past as he paced down the main street, drovers who spent the night in the saloon began to gather outside, shopkeepers began to place items under their windows and the smithy worked up an early morning sweat whilst getting coals so hot they were white. Murphy loved the trail, but loved town life just as much.

He went to the livery stable to get Sea Biscuit and was met by a youth aged about ten. 'Come for your horse, mister?' the boy asked enthusiastically.

'Sure have,' Murphy replied.

'I've cleaned and polished all the leathers, groomed her and last night I gave her a good hard feed.'

Murphy smiled, and thought how the boy was so

much like him at his age. 'Saddle her up,' he said.

The boy worked fast and sharp, and soon Sea Biscuit was ready for action. As Murphy tightened the girth he turned to the boy. 'What's your name, young un?'

'Sam.'

'Well, Sam, here's a dollar for your trouble.'

'A dollar? I've picked her feet, pulled her mane, she looks ready for a church parade.'

Murphy swung onto her back, took the reins in one hand and flicked another dollar at Sam. 'You've got grit, lad, I'll give ya that.'

'Tell you what I'll do,' Sam said mischievously. 'Just for you I'll give a special deal. Twelve dollars for the whole week.'

'Boy – grit's one thing but business is another. Four dollars, seein' as how you've gone and done most of the work she won't need half of all that again.'

'Six dollars,' Sam snapped back.

'Five even.'

'Done!'

Murphy gave a grin, pulled on the reins and swung Sea Biscuit towards the train station. 'Something tells me I have been done,' he muttered.

Coming close to the station, he could see many folk waiting on the platform, so this time he tied Sea Biscuit to the rails outside the building and went to the ticket office, where a smart man dressed in a black uniform was busy filling in a ledger and not looking up at Murphy. Murphy gave a cough but the man paid him no attention. Murphy knocked on the window but nothing. He did it again and still nothing.

'Friend,' he said slowly. 'Has anybody told you that you ain't got no manners?'

The man looked up. 'I've got a railway to run, don't you know? What can I do for you?'

'The Lincoln Flier, when's it due in?' he asked.

'7:10.'

Murphy's eyes went from side to side in embarrassment 'Errr, I've misplaced my pocket watch,' he mumbled.

The man pointed to a clock on the wall between writing. 'The time's right there.'

'Errr, I've lost my spectacles as well.'

The man looked up again. 'Oh, I see, she's due in any time now.'

Murphy nodded thanks. 'Mighty kind,' he drawled.

As he sat on the platform he could see faint traces of smoke coming from the east. Soon the smoke got closer and a steel black engine became visible. The driver sounded its deep horn twice as he released masses of steam and applied the squealing brakes to the wheels. Soon the Flier was panting patiently again as folk rushed on and off. Salesmen with large sample cases, women and children dressed in their Sunday best, farmers with livestock, a gambler, two new cowhands and, to his horror, a lawman wearing a tweed jacket, white pants and a straw bloater. 'Joe Lefors,' he said under his breath as his criminal past

33

took over. Cautiously, he unclipped his .45 and lowered his hat over his eyes. Beneath the brim he saw five heavily armed men with Lefors. They were looking at a piece of paper. *A Wanted poster*, he thought and, not being certain if he was still wanted in other states, he tried to blend in with the background.

After stretching their legs, Lefors and his men got back on the train and Murphy gave a sigh of relief. A whistle blew, the guardsman shouted, 'all aboard!' and the train laboured forwards slowly. Steam engulfed the platform, making it impossible for Murphy to see clearly whom the eight elegant wooden boxes with brass trimmings belonged to; they were placed so as to make a small wall. They all had a matching brass monogram with the initials D.W. on them.

In the calm aftermath, Murphy saw a painfully thin man dancing around them as if he were on hot coals. He was clean-shaven and wore a tight-fitting light blue suit. His neck looked like it was in the process of being strangled by a brown paisley tie, kept neatly in place by a viciously stiff white collar. On his feet were black and white spats with a grey suede anklet above them both, with each anklet fastened by four black velvet buttons. In his right hand was a silver knobbed cane, and with it he clutched a grey top hat with a black silk band. The man was getting quite flustered as he was trying desperately to put his boxes in some semblance of order, but the top ones were much too heavy for him to lift. 'Oafs!' he heard the man grumble. 'Philistines.' The man looked at his gold pocked watch. 'Where is my man?' he muttered as he looked up and spied Murphy. 'I say there, my good man, if you want to earn a shiny sixpence, call me a hackney cab and then come and give me a hand, if you will?'

A cloud of doom entered Murphy's head as he moved forwards slowly. 'You're not Marshal Wheetman . . . Surely to God you're not?'

'The same; who might you be, my man?'

Murphy turned, walked over to a post, took off his hat and headbutted the strut three times. With a pale face, he replaced his hat slowly and turned to face the marshal. 'Me? I'm the mule-headed son of a bitch that two little piggies took to market.'

CHAPTER 4

After the realisation of meeting Marshal Daniel Wheetman had landed firmly on Murphy's mind, he began to gather Daniel's luggage reluctantly, heaving it into a smaller, more compact pile. 'Do be careful, my good man!' the marshal shouted. 'Some of those contain very delicate scientific instruments and I'd look upon it as a personal favour to remember that.'

Murphy gave a grunt, sniffed, cleared his throat and spat on the floor. 'Now, let's get something sorted right from the start.' He fixed Daniel with his best terror stare, the one that worked when he faced down three drunken cowboys looking for a gunfight. 'I'm not your man, I'm your deputy, and I don't tote nothing for you.'

Daniel was completely unmoved and continued to dance around his luggage, pulling and lifting handles like an ant trying to pick up a dead cricket. 'Hmmm?' he asked absentmindedly. 'What did you say?'

'What I was sayin' was that there ain't no way of

getting me to tote and fetch for you. Mores to the point, where's your horse?'

The marshal looked as though he was about to explode when a four-tier stack of luggage began to wobble. As he steadied them with both hands he glanced at Murphy quickly. 'Horse? I don't have a horse. They smell, defecate at will, bite, kick and have such little intelligence so as to render themselves incapable of stopping from running until they drop down dead. Why would I own such a beast?'

Murphy gasped in disbelief. 'What do you mean to say? You don't ride?'

'Of course I ride,' Daniel replied with pride. 'I have ridden in the very best carriages: fine carriages, state carriages. I have taken tea in a royal carriage trimmed with gold and red velvet, but never have I had to stoop so low as to sit on the back of an animal in order to commute from one place to another.' He tilted his head as he took a little time to think and raised his long thin index finger skywards. 'Actually, I tell a lie. There was a time I had the opportunity to ride in a howdah with an Indian prince. The mahout was quite a professional driver as I recollect.'

'What tribe was this mahout from?' Murphy asked. 'By the sounds of it he's Comanche or Apache, maybe even Cheyenne.'

'Tribe? My good man, at the risk of appearing a little didactic – because there's every reason to believe you're a complete ignoramus, but allowing you the benefit of the doubt – I'm talking about India. You know, the one in Asia? The creature in question was an elephant.'

Murphy's face went red with rage as he pointed an accusing finger at the marshal. 'Now, you ain't got no call to insult a fella just for making a mistake, and you ain't got no call to call him an ignoramus or anything else he doesn't understand.' He folded his arms in exasperation and spat. 'Now, all I know is I've got to keep you alive, and saying things like you just said to me to other folk won't make my job any easier. Wait right here, don't talk to anyone until I ride back to town and bring a buggy, then we can get all this stuff – and you – safely to the hotel.' He rose into Sea Biscuit's saddle and pulled the reins back gently. 'Now listen up, Marshal, and listen good: don't talk to anyone until I get back.' He rode a few steps then stopped. 'Don't move now,' he shouted as he pushed his horse forward. 'Don't move, Marshal, don't move now.'

The marshal listened as Murphy's voice disappeared into the distance. 'What a strange fellow,' he muttered.

Before too long, Murphy came clattering back with a horse-drawn buggy he'd obtained from the livery stable, and as soon as he stopped he jumped down and began to lift the marshal's boxes and place them on the flat bed carefully. 'I reckon that's all of 'em, Marshal,' he said whilst thumping down on the spring seat and clasping the reins between his fingers. 'It ain't no royal carriage but it'll take us both to town if you climb on board.'

'Hold it still,' Daniel snapped. 'I'm not quite so used to such primitive transportation.'

Murphy leaned to one side, spat and gave a grin. 'That I'll do, Marshal.'

Gingerly and with great awkwardness, Daniel began to climb on board, and after much ado he managed to sit firmly next to Murphy as Murphy gave the reins a sharp slap.

Whilst the wagon rattled towards town Murphy began to calm down a little, so he looked at the marshal and gave a grin. 'I just for the life of me can't figure out how you managed to get to be a US Marshal. Marshal? You are a Marshal, ain't ya?'

'Oh, I am indeed, and I presume you're my deputy, judging by your interest in my longevity?'

'That's a fact, but why do you talk so funny?'

'Funny? I can assure you, my good man, I speak the Queen's English perfectly, and unfortunately you colonials have managed to make a mockery of such a beautiful language.'

Murphy took off his hat and placed it further to the back of his head. 'Now you may have a burr under your saddle and it ain't goin' to get ya no good at all, take my word for that.'

As Crows Creek became more visible, Murphy looked at Daniel and shook his head. 'I take it you're good with a gun?'

The marshal shook his head. 'Never had one and never will have.'

Murphy pulled hard on the reins. 'You don't have no gun?'

'Well, seeing as you have just committed the crime of using a double negative when you ask if I "don't have no gun" . . . Putting that aside, you are quite correct when you assume I do not have a gun.'

Murphy almost exploded. 'What! You don't have no gun? How the blazes are you goin' to deal with the problems of bein' a marshal when you don't have no gun?'

'Well, I presume this is where you come in. It doesn't take a genius to work out why you are here but I will explain. Firstly, it is obvious from the wear and tear, as well as the smoothness of the butt on your firearm, that you care a great deal about it and on occasion rely upon it. Secondly, you wear your holster quite low down for the weapon to be any-thing other than a self-defence item. I further presume this to be correct due to the fact you tie it closely to your leg, which allows a faster removal from its holster, which I notice is very rigid and hardly the accessory of a man wishing to carry it for use in nothing more than an emergency. Thirdly, your saddle carbine is a Yellowboy, much smoother than a standard weapon. Fourthly, your horse has fine muscle tone and it bears the scars of many a Bovine Ungulate's horn; this is clearly the horse of a master rider. Lastly, you stink like a badger.'

Silence filled the air as Murphy digested what Daniel had said. After a few seconds a grin appeared on his face, which developed into a smile until finally Murphy was completely helpless with laughter, so much so Daniel wondered if he would ever breathe again. After he regained his composure and after wiping the tears from his eyes he slapped the marshal firmly on his back. 'By gobs, man, I've kicked the tar out of men for saying less, but you – you say it in such a way I don't know when you're joshin' or not.'

The marshal looked amazed. 'Oh indeed, I am very serious, but I presume this cowboy lifestyle offers very little opportunity to indulge oneself in some of the more refined habits such as personal hygiene.'

'And I presume the alternative is to smell like a ten-dollar whore because, Marshal, I ain't ever smelled a man so sweet as you.'

Daniel smiled. 'Thank you, my good man. Now, may we proceed to our destination? I have a desire to clean up after my journey.'

Murphy snapped the reins and the horse began to amble towards the livery stable. 'Now, you do just as I'm telling yer, you miserable flea-bitten animal,' Murphy shouted as he yanked the horse's head in the right direction, the direction of the Star Diamond Hotel.

Pulling up outside, Murphy jumped to the ground and tied the reins to the brake. 'Well, Marshal, this is where we live.'

Daniel climbed down carefully and took a long look. 'This will do admirably. Now, if you would be so kind as to bring my luggage and scientific equipment inside. I feel the sun will play havoc with some of the more delicate pieces.'

Murphy gave a howl. 'Now, I thought we'd gotten this sorted out: I don't do nothing in the way of fetchin' and carryin'.' Then he noticed the marshal had already walked away. 'Why, the son of a bitch . . . I orta skin him alive,' he muttered.

As Murphy began to bring in the marshal's things he saw Daniel talking to Clarence and Claude. *I thought those two varmints had never seen the Marshal before?* he thought. Walking over, he began to point. 'Hey, you two, didn't you say you'd never seen the marshal before?'

'Shhh!' one of them said. 'We don't want everyone to know now, do we?'

'No, we certainly do not,' said the other.

Murphy rubbed his chin. 'Which one of you is which?'

'I'm Clarence and this is Claude,' said the one on the left. 'Now, if you wouldn't mind asking again, only this time a little quieter.'

Murphy looked cautiously from side to side and whispered. 'You said you ain't never seen him before and here you are talking and joshin' like you're old pals.'

'We haven't,' Claude replied. 'It was Mr Wheetman who approached us.'

Murphy's eyes narrowed as he looked at Daniel. 'This true, Mr Wheetman?'

'Indeed it is. You see, I was informed that upon my arrival I would be given full instructions by two gentlemen. Two gentlemen who are the living remains of a set of identical triplets.' He took off his hat. 'Gentlemen, may I offer you my condolences on such a recent and tragic loss?'

'My, my,' Clarence replied. 'I had no idea they told you about our very dear brother Clive and his terrible fate.'

'They didn't. All I knew was I would meet identical twins in this very hotel but upon meeting you I deduced your terrible loss within seconds.'

'Really?' Claude asked. 'Please tell us how this trick was done.'

'No trick. I noticed you dress identically, identical to the last degree except for one thing: the rings on your little fingers do not match. You see, you both wear a signet ring on your index finger with the letter C embossed upon the rings. You also wear gold rings on your middle fingers with a symbol suggesting you belong to an ancient organisation dating back to the time of King Solomon. However, gentlemen, one of you wears a further signet ring on your third finger and the other wears the lodge ring, also on his third finger. The only conclusion I can come to is you have lost your other brother, who whilst he was alive he would have worn the same rings exactly the way you two do.'

'That is quite remarkable. 'Clarence gasped. 'But how could you possibly know we only lost dear Clive in the last few months?'

'Ahhh, of course, how very remiss of me,' Daniel mused. 'Obviously they don't quite fit and I notice how you both constantly fondle this third ring, so as to assure yourselves it has not fallen off. You see, I can see you are both quite meticulous in both your habits and dress and have not yet had the opportunity to have those rings made a little smaller, especially as you will not use any old craftsman and therefore must wait until you are both back in Washington.'

'Remarkable. How do you know we frequent Washington?' They both said.

'Unfortunately this is not very remarkable. It says so on the makers label on your brief cases.'

'Well I'll be a hog's grandmother,' Murphy said as he turned away to carry the marshal's luggage upstairs. 'We're in the same room, er, Mr Wheetman,' he shouted.

'Oh dear, this will never do,' Daniel panicked. 'The man is a complete moron, he smells like a sewer, his manners are those of a guttersnipe and I suspect he snores like a trooper.'

'Oh dear ourselves,' Claude began. 'This is the only way we can be certain of your safety; if you have separate rooms, Mr Patterson would not be able to prevent a possible attempt upon your life and Queen Victoria herself has made it perfectly clear what would happen to us if something should happen to you.'

Daniel thought for a while and then accepted his fate for what it was. 'When in Rome . . .' he said philosophically as he sat down with the twins.

'Now, Mr Wheetman,' Claude began, 'this is the situation as we see it. There have been a number of killings in Crows Creek, far more than should be expected for such a town, but nearly all of those killings were in so-called self-defence.'

Daniel raised his right hand to stop Claude.

'When exactly constitutes self-defence?'

'Exactly what it says,' Clarence replied. 'Out here things are a little less formal than in England, but I'm quite certain you're aware of that. However, the ability to carry a firearm in public is quite the norm, as it were, and disagreements over little things such as cheating at cards can be satisfied by a duel.'

'Much as it can be in Great Britain,' Daniel added.

'Quite, but here in the American outback the whole thing is performed in a less honourable way. Therefore, any rules are . . . how can I put this? Quite informal, so to speak. In such a situation, the plea of self-defence can be open to interpretation and left to the judgement of the local sheriff.'

'How does he make such a judgement?' Daniel asked.

'Exactly,' Claude explained. 'If the local sheriff considers the victor in a shooting to be the victim of an attack on his life it is within his jurisdiction to pro-nounce the case to be a simple one of self-defence.'

'This I find to be quite bizarre. . . . What I mean to ask is what criteria does he take into account in order to ascertain the sequence of events?'

'Well,' Clarence continued, 'eyewitness accounts mostly.'

'No ballistic reports or trajectory factors, motives or background history. . . . Surely they have to be taken into account?'

'Not in Crows Creek,' Claude replied.

'I see. Who is the local sheriff?'

'Tom Stoppard, a man of dubious character and

almost certainly in the pocket of the Bannisters, who own just about everything around here.'

'Bannisters?' Murphy added as he sat down. 'I've run into two runts who told me they were the Bannister Boys. I told 'em to git or fight, they chose to git.'

Clarence looked a little concerned. 'It may not be the wisest thing to antagonise the Bannisters, especially as we believe the sheriff Tom Stoppard to be on their payroll.'

Murphy rubbed his chin. 'Tom Stoppard, that name rings a bell. . . . Wait a dog-garn minute, Tom Stoppard used to ride with the Clancy Boys out of New Mexico! I wondered what happened to them. I heard they were both gunned down in Tulsa, then in Carson City and once more in Lincoln, so I guess they're still rustling cattle somewhere. I also thought Tom would still be with 'em.'

'It is a possibility they are still active, as it were,' Clarence explained. 'After my brother and I gathered the facts, we came to the joint conclusion that Tom Stoppard and two other men used to sell horses and cattle to Bannister, and we don't think Bannister was all that concerned where they came from, but that was three years ago. Since then, Bannister's empire has grown.'

'When did Stoppard become sheriff?' Daniel asked.

'One year ago – right after Sheriff Hayes was gunned down, right here in the high street,' the twins replied.

46

'Ah,' interrupted Daniel. 'I read about that in *The Times* – Sheriff Hayes was the President's nephew, if I'm correct?'

'He was indeed.'

'Just a cotton pickin' moment,' Murphy interrupted. 'Where do you two runts come into it and how come you know so much?'

'Oh dear. . . . We wished you wouldn't ask such a thing but I suppose it had to come out,' Claude replied.

'We're government agents,' Clarence said.

'You!' Murphy blurted out. 'Why, you're no bigger than knee-high to a grasshopper.'

'That well may be, but in our line of work it is very often an advantage to appear not what one is but as people perceive us to be.'

'Quite so, brother,' Clarence added, 'and as it is our business to gather the facts involving many situations, we find a smile and good manners win the day every time.'

Daniel sat up. 'How very fascinating. I take it you have an index file for all your cases?'

'Indeed we do. We have files relating to two-hundred-and-sixty-four mystery deaths that have occurred in three states over the last four years,' Claude announced with pride.'

'Two-hundred-and-sixty-four open cases, dear brother; remember we have managed to close eighty seven.'

'You managed to solve eighty-seven?' Daniel asked.

'Not exactly,' Claude replied. 'We managed to

47

close eighty-seven; we only solved five. Well, when we say five, we didn't so much as solve them, they almost solved themselves.'

Daniel looked curious. 'I do not quite understand; either you solved them or not.'

Claude looked at Clarence. 'You see, they were the victims of lynch parties. The local townsfolk took justice into their own hands and hanged the suspects themselves. So, technically, we haven't quite managed to solve any.'

'And that's where the marshal comes in?' Murphy asked.

'Indeed it is, indeed it is,' Clarence replied. 'From what we have been told, you, errr . . . Mr Wheetman . . . have some sort of revolutionary method whereby you manage to ascertain who perpetrated certain crimes just by working things out, and from what we have seen we are very impressed. So this is the plan: both you and Mr Patterson will remain in Crows Creek undercover, so to speak, isn't that correct, brother?'

'Indeed it is. We have documentation, issued by the governor, which officially appoints you, Mr Wheetman, as US State Marshal, and affords you all the powers that accompany such an office. We also have documents that appoint you, Mr Patterson, as Mr Wheetman's deputy, but we are certain you are well aware of that already. However, what you may not be aware of is the necessity to stay undercover until the next incident happens. Isn't that correct, Clarence?'

'Indeed it is, because we feel such an incident will never happen if the nastier elements in this area catch wind of the fact there is a US Marshal in town. Now, as things stand, neither of you are known in Crows Creek, so you will be looked upon with suspicion if we don't come up with a cover story. What do you think, brother?'

'Indeed, such is the case, so we must all put our heads together and think of a scenario that pleases all parties and which will fool the town's residents. Any ideas, gentlemen?'

The quartet sat thinking quietly until Daniel broke the silence. 'I noticed a sign over there near the staircase, asking for bar staff. Perhaps Mr Murphy could turn his hands to that?'

Murphy spluttered. 'I ain't never spent my time on the other side of no saloon counter and I ain't about to start. Besides, I ain't that good at ciphering and such.'

'How quaintly you put things,' Daniel said quietly. 'Surely there can be little difference between buying a drink and selling one, especially when the choice of beverage only ranges from whiskey to beer?'

'What are you getting at?' Murphy asked.

'What I'm trying to explain, if you wouldn't mind listening, is there can be little difference between buying and selling alcohol.'

'Still not with ya.'

Daniel gave a sigh. 'How can I explain it better? Yes, I have it. I presume you know the price of a beer?'

'Of course I do!'

'Equally you know the price of a whiskey.'

'That too.'

'Therefore, if you were to purchase four beers and two whiskeys I presume you would notice if the transaction was correct and not fraudulent.'

'That I would – and any man who tries to cheat me had better know that.'

'So it follows, does it not, that you know how many whiskeys make five or six and how many beers make eight or nine?'

'I guess I do.'

'Eureka! So it must also follow you know how much change you would expect to get from ten dollars if you purchased two whiskeys and three beers?'

'Seven dollars and fifty cents, but what are you trying to get at?'

'Equally, I presume from your time served propping up a bar that you know how much whiskey there should be in an average measure, and indeed how much beer?'

Murphy rubbed his chin in suspicion. 'I guess I do.'

Daniel smiled. 'Oh, come on now, Mr Patterson, don't be modest: I am certain you are quite at home in such an establishment as this.'

Murphy's eyes narrowed. 'What makes you so sure?'

'You keep a certain amount of coins in your right hand waistcoat, correct?'

'Yep.'

'And during my time in your country I have had cause to frequent one or two public houses in order to compare those in Great Britain and those here, and I noticed some interesting mannerisms here that I have not noticed there. One such mannerism found in habitual drinkers is the one of keeping coins in a waistcoat pocket. I also noticed the casual manner in the way the correct coinage is almost flicked onto the bar upon leaving an establishment, almost to show honesty. Equally, it is always gathered up by the bar staff and placed into the till without being counted.'

Murphy leaned forward and placed his right elbow in the table. 'Now get this straight: only a dirty low-down snake would ever cheat in his own saloon, and only the son of a polecat would check a man's honesty.'

'My point entirely,' Daniel announced. 'So it follows neither the licensee nor his or her staff would endeavour to cheat a good customer and visa versa, neither would the patron.'

'I think I know what you mean,' Murphy added.

'May the Lord be praised!' Daniel gasped. 'In summary, you know all there is to know about public houses, you know the prices, the stock, the correct measures and as you admit yourself, no self-respecting customer would endeavour to cheat a landlord and neither would a good landlord cheat a customer. Therefore, you are an ideal candidate for the post in question.'

51

'Indeed he is,' the twins agreed.

Murphy, once again, rubbed his chin. 'I reckon you could be right, but how do I go about getting this job?'

'It's quite simple,' Claude replied. 'Alice McKay knows who you are; she's the one who told us about Tom Stoppard and Bannister so we're certain she would love to hire you. In fact, I'll go and tell her,' Claude rose to his feet and went to see Alice, leaving the other three to discuss matters further.

Daniel shook his head. 'Gentlemen, there is, however, the very serious problem of Mr Patterson's personal hygiene, or rather lack of it.'

'What are you getting at?' Murphy snarled.

'Well, Mr Patterson,' Clarence began. 'Speaking not only for myself and my brother, I am certain Mr Wheetman will agree you do have a lack of respect for cleanliness.'

'Me?' Murphy gasped in disbelief.

Daniel turned towards Murphy and whispered. 'Yes, Deputy; as I pointed out to you earlier, you smell like a badger.'

CHAPTER 5

The time had come for Murphy to take a bath and undergo a change of clothing, and he was about as happy as a gopher in a rattlesnake's den, but the others were adamant it was going to happen. Whilst Daniel remained at the hotel, the twins cajoled Murphy to accompany them to the local bathing house. As they approached the tall wooden building from downwind, the aroma of soap hit Murphy's nostrils and he began to slow down. 'Now, wait a minute, boys,' he began. 'I'm not going to take my clothes off, you do know that?'

Clarence looked up and smiled. 'Mr Patterson, we can assure you there is nothing to worry about. Bella Drinkwater has been running this house for many years now and she's a perfect lady.'

'She's a woman!' Murphy cried. 'I ain't goin' to show what nature intended to be private for no good reason, and a bath ain't no good reason.'

Claude opened the bathing house door and stood back. 'After you, Mr Patterson.' Murphy walked forward like a man going to the gallows. 'Bella will be with us soon; we've no doubt about that.'

After a few moments, the left-hand stall door flew open and a huge woman with shocking red hair emerged. Bella Drinkwater wore men's denim trousers, a red and black lumber shirt held up with a strong pair of black braces, and atop all this she had two grey towels draped over each of her massive arms. 'Well, well, well,' she said with a smile. 'I've just filled this tub with fresh hot water. Are you all going to have a bath? The water will do all three of you. One at a time, you understand?'

'Oh no,' Clarence replied. 'Just Mr Murphy, if that's all right?'

'It'll cost you full price just for one,' she snapped back.

'That will be fine, but I wonder if I could have a private word?'

Claude took Bella to the side of the room and began to whisper in her ear.

Murphy saw this and shifted uneasily from side to side. 'Aw, shucks now,' he muttered. 'I almost forgot, I didn't feed my horse. I'd better go and do it now.'

Before he could move, Bella grabbed his arm and began to drag him into the stall. Murphy had never had this happen to him before and didn't quite know what to do, so he began to resist a little. 'Olga!' Bella shouted as Murphy intensified his resistance. 'Olga, get here now.' At that, an even bigger woman came in from the right and bowled Murphy into the stall without hesitation. Bella followed and slammed the door shut. As the twins looked at one another they could hear Murphy's pleas for mercy.

'Now, ladies,' Murphy shouted. 'Let's not get carried away. Ladies! Don't you touch that . . . Whoa now, what do you think you're . . . Give them back now! I'm not joking; you just do as you're told.' They heard his gun and belt fall to the floor, followed by his boots and, as they continued to strip him, they threw his clothes, one by one, over the top of the door. Murphy's cries fell upon deaf ears as Bella and Olga went about their task. 'This is your last chance,' he cried. 'Don't tear 'em, they were clean on last year . . . They're the only pair I've got that match . . . OK, I give in . . . I'll get in the blasted thing myself.'

The twins crept out into the street slowly and made their way to the general store, where they bought fresh long johns and socks. When they arrived back they passed them to Bella and Olga, and minutes later Murphy emerged like a newly hatched butterfly, proud for all to see. Bella followed. 'I reckon we've got clean duds for your fella. Not new, you understand, but the previous owner won't have no need for 'em since he died last fall.'

Murphy's ears picked up. 'What did he die of?'

'Fell off his horse when he was drunk as a skunk. Broke his neck, the silly beggar,' Bella replied.

'Well, whose were they?'

'My late husband's. He never could ride properly at the best of times, but when he was full of a bottle of whiskey I reckon the Lord must have lost his patience.'

'How much do you require?' Clarence asked.

Bella sniffed. 'There's three good shirts, three pairs of pants, a vest or two, socks, long johns, even his Sunday boots, although I reckon they won't fit: for a big fella he had terribly small feet and, thinking about it, that wasn't the only small thing he had.' She slapped Murphy on the back. 'Not like this'n; he's a ladies man if ever I saw one.'

'That may well be, Bella,' Claude interrupted. 'How much do you require for them all?'

She sniffed again. 'Ten dollars for the lot; you can even have the hope chest they're restin' in. Take it or leave it.'

'We'll take it,' they said as they both handed over five dollars. 'Perhaps Mr Patterson may be allowed to have some in order to get fully dressed?'

'Olga!' she shouted. 'Get Jim's hope chest and bring it here.'

Olga said nothing but strode past them like a grizzly bear, soon to return with a large, very heavy chest, which she slammed on the creaky wooden floor.

Murphy took a suspicious look, rubbed his chin and opened the lid. 'These are real fancy duds!' he shouted like a child at Christmas. 'This black shirt is as good as new, so are the rest, and these here black pants will do just fine.' Quickly, he placed his legs in the pants and pulled them up. Next he donned the shirt, picked up his black leather waistcoat, threw it on and pulled on his boots with great satisfaction. Once again he rummaged in the chest and came out with a white collar. 'Huh?' he said. 'All these here duds are black, exceptin' for this collar.'

Bella sniffed. 'What do ya expect for a preacher?'

'A preacher?' Murphy gasped. 'I'm wearin' a preacher's duds?'

'Sure, why not?' she explained. 'They're in good order, I've boiled washed 'em.' She sniffed again. 'Never thought I'd sell 'em though. Never thought anyone would buy 'em.'

Clarence jumped up. 'You look fine, Mr Patterson. Doesn't he, dear brother?'

'Oh, fine indeed,' Claude agreed. 'Just put your gun-belt back on again and you will feel better.'

As Murphy strapped his gun back on, secretly he quite liked his new look but couldn't admit it. 'I suppose it'll do until I find some new duds.' He looked at the dirty pile on the floor that once was his outfit. 'What'll we do with these?'

'I'll take 'em out back and burn 'em,' Bella said.

'Burn 'em? Hell shit, can't you wash them or something? That shirt alone cost me two dollars.'

'Two dollars?' Bella asked. 'Was that before the war? The best thing to do with these is to burn 'em and burn 'em well.'

Clarence grabbed Claude's arm. 'Come, dear brother; now the next thing we have to do is take Mr Patterson back to the Star Diamond Hotel and show him to Alice McKay. She refused to give him a job until she had seen the finished result, so to speak.'

'I'll send Olga with your things, don't you worry,' Bella added.

'Now you ain't got any call to do that. I can handle things myself,' Murphy said.

'She'll look forward to it, don't you fret yourself. I reckon Olga has taken a right shine to you, big fella.'

Murphy gulped. 'Now you just tell her – so as not to hurt her feelings that is – you tell her I ain't in the market for no woman. I'm a trailhand, a cowboy. Here today and gone tomorrow. Like the wind, I roam the plains.'

Bella laughed. 'That won't bother her none: when Olga wants a fella, Olga gets a fella.'

Murphy grabbed one of the twins. 'Come on, boys, I reckon it's about time to start work.' He placed his hat on his head and tipped it. 'Much obliged, ma'am, but we must be off now.'

The three burst out into the street and made a quick line for the hotel. When inside they noticed the amount of customers had more than doubled since they left and saw Alice as she was taking a tray of drinks to four card-playing cowboys. Murphy waved and in return she cocked her head to beckon him over. Murphy took of his hat and slowly walked over. 'Hang your hat over there, put on a white apron and get behind the bar,' she said.

'Yes, ma'am, sure will,' he replied.

'Hey, what do we call you?' she asked.

'Murphy's just fine, ma'am.'

'Hey, Murphy, you scrub up well. If I wasn't a married woman, I'd have yer.'

Two of the cowboys laughed. 'He smells sweeter than a bride on her wedding night.'

Murphy's face went red with rage but, just as he was about to swing a punch at one cowboy, Alice intervened. 'Hey, Murphy, remember where to hang your hat.'

Murphy's face went from a scowl to a smile in seconds. 'I reckon I do, boys, and what do you think of my fancy duds?'

'Woo-wee! He looks prettier than a cake on Sunday, don't he, boys?' The other three laughed as Murphy nodded, smiled, turned away and headed for the bar where Colin was busy serving drinks.

'It's nice to have ye with us. Murphy, isn't it?' Colin asked.

'The feelings mutual, and Murphy will do real fine.' He grabbed an apron from under the bar, tied it on and smiled at two customers waiting to be served. 'What'll it be, boys?' he asked enthusiastically.

'Two beers,' came one reply.

'Two beers comin' up.' After that, Murphy took to bar keeping like a duck to water as customer after customer were served perfectly.

'Help ye self to a drink whenever ye want,' Colin told him and Murphy smiled at the thought of being in heaven, but his thoughts were interrupted when Alice told him to take a tray of drinks to the four cowboys who had chewed on him. Murphy took a swift drink of whiskey and walked over to their table slowly. 'Howdy, boys – you working round here?'

One of them, who wore a long grey duster, looked at him with snake eyes, the scar on his right cheek almost pointing to his chewed right ear. 'Kind of nosey, ain't we, for a barkeep?'

Murphy smiled as he collected the empty glasses and replaced them with full ones. 'Just bein' friendly, boys; meant no offence.'

One cowboy touched the other's arm. 'He don't mean anything by it, Harvey, he's just doin' his job,' he said.

Harvey scowled. 'Well, I hate it when someone gets to ask too many questions.'

Murphy smiled again. 'Just bein' friendly boys; just doin' my job. Used to be a cowhand myself. Wish I could buy you a drink but this is my first day and I ain't got paid yet.'

Harvey looked up in disbelief. 'You were a cowhand?'

'Since I were a boy of fourteen. Man, the hours are brutal and backbreaking, the days are hot and the nights cold, but not as cold as when I tried a little trapping in Canada.' He wiped their table dry with his towel. 'Those nights were cold; so cold that we had to sleep with the dogs to keep from freezing to death. Some real cold ones were known as "three dog nights". Some were so cold your spit would freeze before it hit the ground.

'Is that a fact?' Harvey said as Murphy began to back off. 'The name's Harvey Pritchard. These two are Tom and Ben Williams, and this feller is Lucky Joe Ballard.'

'Right pleased to meet yer, gents. They call me Murphy,' he smiled at Ballard. 'Lucky Joe, eh? Why do they call you that?'

'That's because I ain't never had any luck. I once won thirty-seven dollars in a poker game then straight away lost it on a bluff hand.'

'That's the story of my life, Joe,' Murphy said. 'When one door opens, another slams in yer face. That's life, I guess.'

Murphy went back behind the bar and once again served drinks like he had done it all his life. 'It takes a big man to do what you just did.' Alice said. 'A mighty big man. At first I thought you were going to wrap a chair around one of their heads but you held back and that takes a mighty big man – you'll do for me, cowboy.'

The rest of the afternoon blended into the evening, which in turn blended into the night, and Murphy loved every minute. He loved the free drinks and found he loved the atmosphere, and he loved the smell of the place so much he almost forgot why he was there. The hour was late and everyone had left except for the four cowboys and a couple of gamblers at the table. 'Come on, boys,' Alice shouted. 'Drink up now, if you please.' She asked Murphy to collect their glasses and see them out.

Murphy went over to the table and began to pick up the drinks. 'Nice to meet you, boys, but it's time to lock the doors now if you don't mind.'

The cowboys all stood up and shuffled away from the table slowly. 'Let's get back to the ranch, boys,' Harvey said.

Murphy smiled. 'Long drive, boys?' he asked.

'Just as far as the Parker ranch, 'bout an hour's

ride north,' Lucky Joe answered.

Murphy slapped him on the back and stumbled onto his boot. 'Hey, sorry, Lucky Joe. Maybe I should take a little water with it, but don't stay away now.' He looked puzzled as he locked the doors behind them and went on to collect more glasses. 'The Parker range, ma'am, is it a big spread?' he shouted.

Alice looked concerned. 'Not very when compared to the Bannister spread, but big enough for Bannister to leave them alone. Why do you ask?'

'Oh, there was something about those boys that told there was more to their scratching than a couple of fleas.'

'What do you mean?'

'Well, they were tooled up enough to fight a war, the one wearing that duster had a pair of .45s, plus I saw the handle of the .38 next to his vest. The one called Lucky Joe wore a shoulder holster as well as carrying a knife down his boot. I felt the holster as I slapped him friendly like, and the knife as I accidentally stumbled on his boot.'

'Hey, cowboy, where did you learn that?'

'Let's just call it experience, ma'am.'

CHAPTER 6

In the cool light of day, Murphy realised a few things. He pulled up the bedroom drapes and looked out into the street below. He knew Marshal Wheetman was clever but was likely to get his head blown off by the first cowboy he spoke down to. He also knew the twins were not quite what he first thought they were. He knew what it felt like to be clean. He knew he liked to keep bar, but most of all he knew the marshal snored louder than anybody else he had ever heard. The noise Daniel produced was so loud that the china washbasin vibrated like a church bell on a Sunday morning. In order to stop it from fragmenting into a thousand pieces, Murphy had to place his boots inside it to stop the resonance.

Sometime in the early hours of the morning, Murphy managed to drop off into a deep sleep. It was a sleep without dreams, a sleep almost of the dead, but now he was awake and having his regular early morning scratch as he looked out of the window. He smiled as he saw two children running with hoops. In the distance he could see Sea Biscuit being groomed outside the livery stable, but his sunny attitude broke down into panic when he saw the marshal walking towards Katie's Eating House.

'What in blazes. . . . How did he do that? I didn't hear a thing. Why, he's more slippery than an eel in a bucket of hog's grease,' he said to himself as he bounced around on one leg trying to put his pants on. Hurrying to get dressed, he ran down the stairs whilst carrying his carved leather rig over his shoulder and holding his boots in his teeth. Outside he sat on the high walk and finished dressing before running after Daniel. 'Marshal!' he shouted, as Daniel was about to enter Katie's. 'Hell's teeth,' he mumbled as he hurried forward. 'Errr, Mr Wheetman,' he shouted louder, and this time he got Daniel's attention. He turned to see who wanted him.

Daniel took a second look, hardly able to believe Murphy was smart and clean. 'My, my,' he said as Murphy drew close. 'I can see an awful lot has taken place since we last met. Could it be an angel of mercy has answered my prayers?'

'You ought not to go anywhere in town without me seein' as it's OK first.'

Daniel gave an unforgiving tut. 'I see the angel restricted its attentions to your appearance and not your vocabulary.' He gave a sigh. 'I presume from your garbled statement you do not wish that I should go anywhere in Crows Creek without your permission. Is this correct?'

'That's about the size on it.'

'Well, shall I take it that I have your approval to enter this eating house?'

Murphy moved Daniel aside gently, reached for the door handle, gave it a twist and went inside to check if the Bannister Boys or any other shady looking characters were in there. 'It seems OK,' he drawled.

'Thank you,' Daniel said as he nodded his false approval. 'You appear to be somewhat overzealous with your vocation, Mr Patterson.'

'I ain't taking no chances, that's all.'

Once again Daniel gave a sigh. 'At the risk of confusing you, I will keep this quite simple. If we are both going to share portions of our lives in one another's company, I would appreciate it if you would try not to strangle the Queen's English into some sort of undecipherable gobbledegook.'

Murphy began to laugh. 'Why, you really do take the biscuit with all your fancy talk. I swear I ain't never done heard anyone speak right and proper the way you do. You should be on the stage, mister.'

Daniel looked skywards. 'Why does God give nuts to toothless children?' he asked as he went inside.

Once again, Katie's voice came from the back. 'Whoever that is, just help yourself to coffee; it's on the stove over yon', and I'll be with you in a jiffy.'

'Thank you kindly, ma'am,' Murphy replied.

Katie came out from the back with wide eyes as she wrung her hands on her pinafore. 'You again?' she snapped. 'Don't start trouble like you did yesterday.

I'm not in the mood for it, especially since Myrtle May ran off with that fancy salesman last week.'

Murphy took off his hat and hung it on the stand near the door. 'Now that ain't right,' he protested. 'Those boys were stickin' in my craw.'

'That ain't no call to go and threaten to shoot up my eating house.'

Daniel gave another sigh. 'Doesn't anyone in this town know anything about the rules of grammar?'

Katie's eyes turned to look at Daniel. 'Who are you?' she said accusingly.

'Madam,' he began. 'I am but a simple man who wishes to partake of a little meal. This is not to intimate your meals are simple by way of lack of imagination or have limited ingredients. I mean only to ask for English Tea accompanied by two lightly boiled eggs and three slices of toast, lightly done on both sides, if you please.'

Katie shuffled uneasily. 'Pancakes, bacon, eggs and coffee is all you can have until dinnertime. Take it or leave it.'

'What!' exclaimed Daniel as Murphy interrupted.

'That'll do just fine, ma'am, and if'n it's alright we'll sit over there so we can keep an eye on the door.'

'You expecting anyone?' she snapped again.

'Oh no, ma'am, we . . . errr . . . just like to greet folk with a nice smile as they come in. We think it's kinda more friendly, like.'

Katie pointed to Daniel. 'And what about your funny friend?'

'He'll have the same, ma'am.'

66

'Really, I must protest,' Daniel gasped, but Murphy put his hand on his shoulder to calm him down.

'Just simmer down, Marshal,' he whispered. 'We ain't supposed to be standin' out as it were, we're supposed to blend, remember?'

'I merely want boiled eggs, tea and toast,' Daniel said through gritted teeth. 'Why should anyone have to wait until this evening to experience a change of menu?'

'You don't,' Murphy replied. 'Just until dinner.'

'Exactly! Evening,' Daniel explained.

'Dinner ain't in the evening – that's supper.'

Daniel shook his head. 'The order of events is as thus: morning tea, or breakfast if you prefer, followed by lunch, which in turn is followed by afternoon tea, and finally we have dinner.'

Murphy smiled. 'That's maybe how things are in England, but here we have breakfast, dinner and supper. Take it or leave it.'

Just then the door opened and a fat, balding man wearing dungarees and a leather apron came in. 'Katie,' he said merrily. 'How are you, my precious? I'll get my own coffee whilst you rustle me up two rounds of pancakes and double bacon and eggs, if that's fine with you?'

'Henry Copeland,' she replied. 'Don't you try smooth-talking me just so I will serve you first. Wipe your feet and sit down.'

His ruddy complexion shone when he smiled. 'Marry me, Katie, and make me the happiest blacksmith in the whole wide world.'

'Stop all that blather. Things are not as fast as they were when Myrtle May was around and you know that.'

'You heard from her?' he asked.

'Not so much as a single word – and after all I did for that ungrateful girl.' She turned and headed for the kitchen. 'You gents just have to wait.'

In the silence that followed, Murphy nodded to the blacksmith, who replied in turn. 'You boys here on business?' Henry asked.

'Nope,' Murphy replied. 'I'm the new barkeep at the Star Diamond Hotel. Murphy's the name.'

'And you, stranger?'

'I'm a government man,' Daniel replied as Murphy almost choked on his coffee.

'Government man?' the blacksmith asked. 'What exactly does that mean?'

Murphy held his breath, waiting for Daniel's reply. 'Land survey,' he explained casually. 'I have been empowered to draw up a register of all the businesses, farms and resources available in and around Crows Creek, as well as complete a census.'

'What in tarnation is a census?' Henry asked.

'A census is a register of all those who reside here, their names, occupations and ages; it is quite simple.'

'Why do you have to do that?'

'I am not at liberty to divulge the purpose behind such a register except to assure everyone there is nothing sinister about it.'

Henry gave sly look to his left. 'Well, I reckon it'll be fine, but there are one or two might not agree. I don't fancy your job, errr, Mister. . . ?'

'Wheetman's the name. Daniel Wheetman at your service, sir.'

'You sure are a polite one, though,' Henry said. 'Maybe you won't get on folk's craw but I'll stick to shoein' horses and such like.'

Once again the door opened, and two ladies wearing gingham dresses came in and sat down without saying a word.

'Ladies,' Henry said as he tipped them a wink. 'These two are new in town. One works at the Star Diamond, and this other fella here is a government man; he's here to find out who's who in Crows Creek. Ain't that a fact?'

Daniel sniffed his coffee with disgust and pushed it away. 'That is correct sir, but I must point out, the whole thing is quite informal and furthermore in its trial stage.'

Murphy grabbed Daniel's arm. 'What in tarnation are you up to?' he whispered.

'Quite simple,' he began. 'My presence in this town will not be unnoticed and the thought of me being some sort of government man will provide a perfect alibi should the need exist for me to ask a few questions.'

Murphy grinned. 'You sure are one clever son of gun, that right you are.'

After a while of silence, the door opened again and two cowboys came in, wiping their feet and tapping the dust off their chaps. In turn, they hung their hats up and smiled at the other five. 'Katie!'

one of them shouted pleasantly. 'It's Josh and Stewart.'

'You know where the coffee is, boys,' came her reply. 'I'll be with you in a minute.'

The cowboys smiled, nodded at the others and sat down.

'This here fella is a government man,' Henry said with pride. 'He's here to find out what we're up to and who we are.'

'That a fact?' Josh said. 'Pleased to meet ya, sir.'

'The feeling is mutual, gentlemen,' Daniel replied as Katie came through the door with three plates of pancakes.

'You boys work around here, I take it?' Murphy asked.

'Over at the Parker ranch,' Josh replied casually.

'I met some other cowboys who work there, one by the name of Harvey Pritchard.'

'He works for Bannister and that's why we're in town. Bannister has a proposition for us. We'll listen to it but the Parkers are good folk to work for.'

'The hell you say?'

'That's a fact,' Josh said.

Again, Katie came back and swept through the room, dropping off a plate in front of Daniel, Murphy and Henry skilfully before she glided back towards the kitchen. Murphy's eyes lit up. 'Pancakes and syrup,' he said as he began to drown them with the sweet sauce.

In contrast, Daniel cut a small slice out of one and popped it in his mouth. 'Awful!' he gasped.

'Oh shucks now, they ain't so bad.'

'How in hell would you know? Yours are covered in that sweet sickly syrup; how on earth would you know what they taste like?' Daniel looked at Henry, who was shovelling his into his cavernous mouth as quick as possible. 'Excuse me, my good man, would you care to have mine? You appear to be enjoying them.'

With his mouth full, Henry stood up, came over to Daniel and took his plate with a smile and a nod. 'What you doin'?' hissed Murphy. 'You don't want to go about hurtin' anyone's feelings, especially a lady's.'

'Nonsense. A little criticism never hurt anyone. Besides, they are not seasoned, they are much too thick and quite soggy,' Daniel replied.

'Hey, Katie! This here Englishman doesn't like your cooking,' Henry shouted mischievously.

Seconds later an enraged Katie came back into the room, and with her hands placed firmly on her hips asked, 'And I think his high and mighty self could do better?'

'Of course I could,' Daniel replied casually. 'I have prepared dishes for those with the most discerning palate and, may I state, without complaint.'

Katie went quiet and then asked 'Can you bake?'

'Of course I can bake, but I must admit my passion is cakes, I believe there should be a cake for all occasions.'

'Can you make a cherry pie?' she asked.

'Cakes, pies, soufflés, meringues, marzipan, trifles and crêpes are just some of the desserts I can make.'

71

Katie peered at Daniel. 'You fancy fillin' in for Myrtle May?'

Daniel thought for a while and smiled. 'Madam, I would consider it an honour to be able to apply my services if it increases the quality of your cuisine.'

Murphy laughed. 'He sure do talk funny, don't he just?'

Henry leant forwards on his table. 'You joshin', mister?'

Daniel said nothing as Murphy whispered. 'He wants to know if you're telling the truth, Mr Wheetman.'

'The truth? Of course I am telling the truth; why ever should I lie?'

'The pay is three dollars a day. Take it or leave it?'

'Madam, any monetary remuneration is quite unnecessary,' he explained.

Once again the door opened and Sheriff Tom Stoppard walked in. Murphy wasn't quite certain if he'd be recognized or not, so he dropped his head a little. The sheriff sat down with the cowboys Josh and Stewart and they began to mumble to each other.

'Hey, Sheriff,' Henry said out loud. 'This here fella says he's a government man and can cook and bake like the sweetest little lady I could ever imagine.'

The sheriff stopped talking and looked at Daniel. 'Government man? Nobody told me anything about no government man.'

'I'm here to conduct a simple census – more of a report, if you will – about who does what in Crows Creek. It is quite a routine matter; I am surprised you have never heard of it before. Why, in the larger cities it has been going on for years now.'

'But you're English,' the sheriff said suspiciously.

'Indeed I am, and that is the very heart of the matter, because in England there have been regular census reports since the Doomsday Book in the eleventh century.'

The sheriff looked beyond Daniel. 'Hey, you, stranger,' he said out loud. 'Have I seen you before?'

'I expect you have, Sheriff,' Daniel interrupted. 'My friend here is what you refer to as a barkeep at the Star Diamond Hotel. You may have seen him there?'

The sheriff thought for a while. 'Oh yes, I remember. Nice to have you in town, errr, Mr. . . ?'

'Patterson. John Samuel Patterson.'

CHAPTER 7

Breakfast at Katie's went fairly well. Daniel had had the chance to see Tom Stoppard and introduce himself as a government employee conducting a census. His passion for fine foods meant he would take advantage of Kate's offer of him making some desserts, plus he could escape typical western foods and cook some palatable dishes for himself, but Murphy didn't share his verdict on the day.

As they walked back towards the hotel, Murphy explained his concerns. 'I wonder if the sheriff recognized me from the days when I rode the trail?'

'Ah, Tom Stoppard, the reformed outlaw and probable partner in crime with Bannister?'

'The same,' Murphy replied.

'Almost certainly he did not. You see, I have taken the trouble to study what is known as body language, and the thing about body language is it has a universal application. Take, for instance, a Sikh, now a typical gentleman with—'

'Whoa, right there,' Murphy interrupted. 'What in

74

the name of Moses is a Sikh?'

'A Sikh? Ah, well, he or she is a member of a certain faith. Every male has sworn never to have his hair cut so he has to wear a turban. Before you ask, a turban is a sort of cloth that is wrapped around their head. However, in their country, in order to indicate the answer "no" with their head, they would nod, and "yes" would be performed with a sideways movement, rather like our "no" but in reverse. Are you with me so far?'

Murphy nodded.

'Precisely. If you were in the land of the Sikhs you would have just said no. I use this example to explain we are not talking about customs but body language, and the two are completely unrelated. Body language is an unconscious or involuntary bodily action that gives away our true feelings.'

'The hell you say?'

'Oh, I do, my dear fellow, and I can put it quite simply. When a person, possibly a lady, does not wish to converse with someone, do you notice her posture?'

'You mean she goes all ornery?'

'Well, in a way I do mean that, but take a typical action: if she were in a sitting position, she would turn slightly away, cross her legs, fold her arms and raise her head in a superior fashion.'

'That's what Rebecca Smith did to me at the barn dance two years ago. I thought she'd got a stiff neck or something, but after what you have just told me it explains why she went off with that rat Jed Warren, and after I bought her flowers and candy too.'

'Understanding body language could have saved you the cost of those flowers and chocolates, and possibly the embarrassment of being rejected,' Daniel explained.

Murphy grinned. 'Not really. Cynthia Calvert saw what happened and took to comforting me right good; that's a night I'll never forget.'

'Oh, I see. Well, do you understand the general gist of my lesson?'

Murphy nodded.

'Well, the study of body language can be a very useful tool when it comes to establishing what a person really means. Now in the case of Sheriff Stoppard, he did not show any signs of telling a lie when he agreed to having seen you in the Star Diamond Hotel: he did not touch his nose, cover his mouth, turn his gaze to the left, hesitate or stutter. No, my good man, I put the suggestion in his head as to him having seen you working in the hotel and not before.'

Murphy rubbed his chin. 'I reckon I can't truly say I've seen him before myself; it just worried me we may have ridden together.'

'There was something else I managed to discover. Nothing much, but something nonetheless.'

'What was that?'

'The man is scared of something.'

'Well, he's the sheriff, and the last one was gunned down according to what I heard.'

Daniel shook his head. 'No, this is different. This is something real and now. Something has either happened or is about to happen, and you can tell from the way he sat, almost ready to spring up and deal with something. His eyes were flickering from side to side, which is the result of fear. Stress would be a by-product of succeeding a sheriff whose term of office ended with his unfortunate demise.'

'I think I understand,' Murphy mumbled.

'Good man. Now, from what I can ascertain, Tom Stoppard had a hand in the killing of the previous sheriff, either directly or indirectly, so he must feel quite confident with the knowledge it was he or Bannister who perpetrated the crime and thus lower the stress factor associated with his position as town sheriff. But fear is something one can focus on, something here and now, and it is my consideration that Tom Stoppard is frightened about something about to happen.'

Murphy laughed. 'You keep thinking, Marshal, and I'll watch your back.'

'Whilst I'm thinking, I must ask the obvious question of your attire and how you came by it.'

'Well, I told the twins it was about time I smartened myself up a bit, so I went to the bathhouse to get all slicked up. The lady there was very helpful and showed me a clean tub with lots of hot water. She gave me a soap and towel and left me to soak. After I was all cleaned up, she took a kinda shine to me and gave me some new duds that belonged to her last husband – he left her two years ago, ran away to New Orleans with a saloon girl – and these are some of the fancy duds I'm wearin' now.'

'And where are the rest?' Daniel asked.

Suddenly Murphy's face went white. 'Oh, good Lord, they're bein' brought over by Olga.'

'Olga?' Daniel asked.

'Never mind,' Murphy snapped. 'Well, I suppose there's no problem, but Olga took a kinda shine to me as well.'

'You know, Deputy, you touched your nose twice, covered you mouth once and looked to the left once whilst you were telling me the full and factual account of your bath and, coupled with the fact your pupils dilated when you mentioned Olga, I suspect there is quite a lot more to this scenario than you divulged. And as for working in the barroom?'

'Yep, as soon as I got back, Alice grabbed me and begged for my help. I worked all evening and half the night; I sure was plum tuckered out when I went upstairs.'

'And I presume I was asleep?' Daniel asked.

'Like you was dead,' Murphy replied. 'I swear I ain't never known a man snore like you do.'

'Mr Patterson, I do not see the point you are making: dead men do not snore.'

'Marshal, you snore louder than a donkey brays.'

'What nonsense! A gentleman never snores.'

As soon as they entered the hotel, they were met by an excited Olga. She stood six feet tall and was wearing a voluminous pink Sunday dress with white frills running around every edge. Her blonde pig-tailed hair was set in ringlets that looked like doughnuts glued to either side of her head. 'My

Murphy!' she screamed in her Viking accent. 'He is such a very big man.' She bounced forward, took him in a bear hug and lifted all six foot four inches of him off the ground like he was made of feathers. 'And he is my man.' She kissed him on the cheek. 'My very big man.' Next she rubbed his belly. 'First I think I have to feed you up a little.'

'Olga!' he pleaded. 'You've got it wrong, I'm a trail bum, a lousy cowhand. I ain't no woman's man.'

'A voman's place is vizz her man, no matter vere that is.' She took his cheeks in both hands and shook his face. 'I have put your luggage in your room and now I have vork to do, but I shall be back.' And with that, she left, leaving Murphy speechless.

CHAPTER 8

Two weeks passed by. The twins had left Crows Creek, leaving Murphy and Daniel to go about their varying lifestyles. Between carrying out scientific experiments and making observations around town, the marshal took the time to bake some wonderful desserts in Katie's Eating House, and the new recipe pancakes became Katie's bestseller – so much so that folk were talking about them in the next valley. Murphy worked in the bar and tried in vain to avoid Olga but she hung on to him like a limpet. Being a devout catholic, Olga's sexual demands upon Murphy were non-existent; she was saving herself until they became 'man and vife'. Murphy had little to say in the matter, but there was one good thing to come out of the one-sided romance, which was that Olga would beat the tar out of anyone who so much as looked at Murphy in a funny way. One night in the hotel, there were three cowhands who happened to laugh as Murphy walked past. Olga thought they were poking fun at him and, according to Alice, she 'bust them up real good'.

Murphy could go about town strutting like a bantam cock: wherever he went he drew respect. At work, nobody dared chew on him for fear of Olga's retribution.

Daniel spent the evenings in their room, either reading or trying out some scientific experiment or other, until two shots rang out from the Golden Shoe saloon across the street one night.

Immediately, Daniel came running downstairs and out into the street. Murphy grabbed the scattergun from behind the bar and ran after him. The first thing Daniel saw was a small crowd of onlookers outside the saloon, hustling and bustling to see what had happened. He forced his way through to see the sheriff holding two men at gunpoint and the body of a dead man lying next to a tumbled-over chair. It was obvious the man had just been shot and the smell of cordite hung heavy in the air. While the onlookers jabbered like a troop of monkeys, Daniel took his place in the crowd.

The sheriff held up his free hand and shouted, 'Settle down now, settle down; let's have some quiet.' The crowd went silent as the sheriff's gaze went about the room. 'Now,' he began. 'Why doesn't someone tell me what went on?'

'It was self-defence, Sheriff,' said a short, scruffy, red-haired, unshaven man with wild eyes. 'He pulled a gun on my partner, Jed, but Jed managed to get him first.'

The sheriff pointed his gun at the taller of the two.

'Are you Jed?' The man nodded his head. 'Suppose you tell me what happened.'

The tall man looked like a mountain, slim and lithe with a rugged complexion. 'Well, it's just as Red said: he went for his gun and I got the drop on him. Maybe he had a misfire. Who knows?'

Stoppard looked at the body on the floor. 'Anybody know who he is?' he asked.

'That's Luke Silverton; he owns Low Grange, about ten miles out of town,' one onlooker said.

'Did anyone see what happened?' the sheriff asked.

'We did, Sheriff,' replied Joe Ballard and Tom Williams. They were two of the four cowboys that chewed on Murphy in the Star Diamond. 'It's just as this man said: this here fella on the floor stood up and pulled his gun first. Ain't that so, Joe?'

'I reckon it is, sir. He pulled his gun but this gent got the better of him and shot him twice. You can see his gun on the floor, right next to where he landed.'

The sheriff looked around. 'Did anyone else see what went on?' he pointed to a man standing close by. 'And you, did you see anything?' The man shook his head then looked to the ground. The sheriff asked someone else who also shook his head.

'I tell ya, Sheriff, it was a case of self-defence,' Red said.

The sheriff put his gun away and grunted. 'Someone give me a hand with the body. You four will have to come to the jail and give me a statement, but I guess it's a case of self-defence.'

Daniel rushed forward. 'Don't anyone touch that body!' he shouted. 'Don't anyone move.'

The sheriff screwed up his face. 'Says who?'

Murphy's voice growled from behind his scatter-gun. 'Says Marshal Wheetman, that's who.'

The sheriff pointed at Daniel. 'Him? He's a marshal?'

'I reckon he is, and I'm his deputy,' Murphy drawled.

Daniel danced with excitement. 'Tally ho!' he shouted. 'The chase is on,' he pointed to Murphy hurriedly. 'Deputy, whatever you do, make certain nobody moves. Help him, Sheriff, whilst I nip and get my bag.'

The marshal ran across the street like a naughty schoolboy playing hooky, and soon returned with a large leather bag, which he placed on the table next to the body. 'Now,' he said, pointing to Red and Jed. 'Will you gentlemen be so kind as to stand exactly where you were when the incident took place?'

'We was right here,' Jed replied.

'And you two witnesses, where were you at the time when the shots went off?' Daniel asked.

'Sitting over there, next to the piano,' Lucky Joe replied.

'Hmm, I see.' He looked at the crowd. 'I wonder if everyone could go and stand or sit in the place they occupied when the shots were fired.' The crowd moved about under an almost silent mumble. 'Very well. Now, let us see what we shall see, shall we?'

Daniel noticed Luke Silverton was lying flat on his

back with both arms above his head. 'That's very odd,' he observed. 'I see his arms are above his head, and yet his supposed weapon is on the floor in-between his legs. I also notice he does not wear a gun-belt or holster.' Daniel pointed to tall Jed. 'When you fired the shot, what position were you in?'

'I don't gets ya,' Jed replied.

'What I mean to ask is, were you standing or sitting? Did you shoot from the hip or with one arm outstretched?'

'I don't rightly recollect; it all happened so fast. All I know is he went for his gun first.'

Daniel smiled at Jed. 'Quite so, sir, but can you remember if he was sitting or standing when he produced his pistol?'

'I can remember, Marshal,' Red interrupted. 'He was sitting, and as he stood up he pulled his pistol.'

The sheriff butted in. 'Wait a cotton pickin' moment. How do we know you're a real marshal? You're the government man come here for some survey or other, and he's just a barkeep.'

'Sheriff, I realise this may be difficult, but you will have to trust me on this matter. However, in our room we have all the necessary paperwork to prove we are exactly who we say we are, but right now I have better things to occupy my time, namely getting down to what has actually happened.'

Murphy stepped closer. 'And I've got this scatter-gun to explain things until we prove who we say we are.'

'And I have zis gun as vell.'

Murphy gave a sigh. 'Olga, what in the name of hell are you doin' here?'

'I heard, I saw, and I come to protect my man.' Olga stood proud and strong, holding a sawn-off double-barrelled Danish shotgun of enormous proportions like it was a toy.

Daniel put on a pair of white gloves, and looked at Jed. 'Now sir, may I have your weapon?' Jed grumbled but passed it to him reluctantly. Next he looked at Red. 'And may I have yours also?' Red did the same. Daniel placed both guns on a vacant table next to him. 'Now, I presume you were both sitting at the same table as the deceased?' They nodded. 'And judging by those playing cards placed there you were indulging yourself in a game?'

'Yep,' Jed replied.

'And that was the cause of it, Marshal,' Red added. 'That low-down skunk was cheatin' and when we told him so he stood up and pulled a gun.'

Daniel looked at the table. 'I see there are two hands here. Which one is yours?' he asked, pointing to Red.

'The one on the left. The other's Jed's.'

Daniel turned to the sheriff. 'You notice, Sheriff, their cards have been placed face down on the table but those belonging to Mr Silverton are scattered over the floor.'

'And your point is?' the sheriff asked.

'The point I make is that if the deceased was clutching a hand of cards with one hand and picking them up with the other, he could hardly have been holding a gun, so the weapon must have been either on his lap or tucked in his belt.'

'It was in his belt, Sheriff,' Jed insisted.

'In his belt, sir?' Daniel asked. 'But a moment ago you said it all happened so fast and you could not remember if you shot him from the hip or with your arm outstretched.'

Jed shuffled nervously. 'Well, it did happen fast, but some of it's comin' back to me. I did shoot from the hip and he had a gun in his belt.'

'You are certain?'

'Yep.'

'Why were neither of you holding cards, or am I to presume you both placed them on the table because you were about to accuse the deceased of cheating?' Daniel asked.

'What are you getting at?' Red asked.

'What I am "getting at" as you put it, is that it rather looks as though you were both ready to pull your pistols and shoot this poor man.' Daniel pointed to two glasses on the table. 'Are these yours?'

'Yep,' Jed said.

'And I presume the one on the right is yours?'

'Yep.'

Daniel took out some white powder, a soft brush and began to brush the powder onto the sides of the glasses. Next he took out a large magnifying glass and examined both of the drinking glasses. 'Hmmm, that's quite interesting.' He shuffled over to the dead body and dusted the gun lying between his legs. 'Aha, just as I thought,' he said. Next he dusted the dead man's glass and examined the powder marks.

'Sheriff,' he began. 'I spent some time in India learning their forensic techniques. Over there they use fingerprints to establish who has touched a certain object and thus they taught me how to perform this procedure. You see everyone's fingerprints are unique. They cannot be changed, erased or filed away: they stay the same all one's life.

'Now, with the use of this magnifying glass and dusting powder, I have compared the fingerprints on those glasses with the fingerprints on Mr Silverton's gun and thus established who touched it last – or indeed, who has touched it at all – and I can state without any doubt that the only person to have touched that gun was this gentleman here.' He pointed to Red. 'In fact, I can go on to further state that there is not one single fingerprint on the gun which belongs to the deceased. The poor man never held it, so I cannot see how he could have pulled it from his belt or grabbed it from his lap, as these gentlemen claim.'

The sheriff objected. 'How do we know you're telling the truth? I ain't never heard of fingerprints.'

'But I guarantee you have all seen them for yourselves on every glass, mirror or windowpane, and I can assure you every fingerprint is quite unique.'

Some of the crowd looked at one another and nodded their heads in agreement as the sheriff scratched his head. 'Every one is different, you say?'

The sheriff's question made Daniel almost giddy with excitement. 'Yes, every single fingerprint is different, but you must allow me to show you.' He rushed over to the bar and returned with two freshly cleaned whiskey glasses, which he held up in the air so his audience could see. Next he gave one to the sheriff. 'Now if you would pretend to take a drink from this glass and place it on the table right here.' The sheriff did as he was asked. 'Next, I shall remove one glove and emulate the sheriff's actions, thus,' Daniel took out his brush and dusted both glasses gently. 'Now, sir, you can plainly see with the naked eye the patterns that have formed, and those patterns are made by the little swirls found on the fingertips of humans.' He looked at the crowd. 'In the interest of science, check to see if your own fingerprints are the same as the person next to you and I am certain they will not be.'

'By gobs, you're right, Marshal,' Murphy added. 'You certainly are a clever son of a gun.'

'Now, Sheriff, if you would so good as to take this magnifying glass and examine those prints on your glass and those on mine, you will see they are quite different.'

After the sheriff did as he was asked he gave a nod. 'That they are,' he confirmed.

Daniel, now filled with self-indulgent pride, continued. 'Now try it again with the prints on this man's glass and the gun on the floor and see if you concur with my findings.'

Reluctantly, the sheriff checked both items and confirmed his findings with a nod. 'They are the same.'

Rather like a Victorian melodrama, a gasp came

from the crowd.

'Well, unfortunately, the use of fingerprint information in a trial is not accepted in either Great Britain or the United States, but this brings me to my next experiment.' Rather like a sideshow salesman, he proudly produced a small atomiser. 'Ladies and gentlemen, if I spray the solution in this atomiser in the area of the gun blast, a reaction will occur when the solution meets spent gunpowder.' He sprayed towards the dead body. 'Immediately you see the solution turns red wherever it comes into contact with cordite. I ask you to notice the table, the cards, and the floor have all turned red, but take a note of the fact there is no red colouration on the lower half of Luke Silverton; which means he was sitting at the time he was shot.' He sprayed Luke's palms. 'Just as I suspected, they stain red, as do the cards he was holding. As for the gun, it also stains red, but only on one side. Thus, I deduce it was thrown at the deceased just before the first shot happened,' Daniel pointed to Jed and Red. 'This is a case of premeditated murder performed by these two men. They gunned down an innocent man wilfully and deliberately, for what reason I do not know. Be certain, gentlemen, I will discover the real motive for the killing of Luke Silverton.'

Jed's eyes moved from side to side as he began to panic. His breathing intensified as he realised their plan had gone wrong. 'It wasn't my idea; we were forced to do it.'

'Shut your mouth, you fool!' Red shouted as he

made a grab for his gun, but Murphy stopped him with one barrel straight into his chest. Red was almost dead before he hit the ground.

Murphy fixed the other killer with steely eyes. 'I've still got a barrel left if you want it, mister?' he said.

The marshal looked at Murphy in desperation and sighed. 'You have just killed that man.'

'Sure have, Marshal. I reckon I don't know any way of shootin' a man at close range with a scattergun and only winging him.'

'What about his legs? You could have shot his legs or given him a warning shot across the bows,' Daniel gasped.

Murphy grinned. 'Look, Marshal, you do your job and I'll do mine. I ain't takin' any chances. What if he'd have grabbed his gun and shot you? Where would I have been then?'

'He was a witness,' Wheetman snapped.

'Why, of all the ungrateful sons of bitches I have ever come across, you have to be at the top of the list,' Murphy snapped back. 'And it's all your fault.'

'My fault? How on earth can you lay the blame at my door?'

'That there body language: I knew he was goin' to go for his gun when I saw his left eye a-quiverin'.'

Daniel grasped his head in disbelief. 'For your information, he had a nervous tick in his left eye. He couldn't help it, didn't you notice it?'

'How was I to know? I ain't no doctor.'

'My dear man, if all you are going to do is indiscriminately kill every Tom, Dick or Harry who happens to have some sort of nervous disorder some-time before they have had a proper trial, there would be no need for the justice system. I presume if it were to be left to you and your "shoot on sight" policy, justice would be dispensed by morons at the other end of the barrel of a gun.'

Murphy's eyes tightened. 'There you go again with all that "my dear man" shit, and whilst I'm talking, I got to ask: who are you calling a moron? I ain't certain what it means but what I does know it ain't good.'

Whilst Murphy and Daniel were bickering, the sheriff and Jed looked at one another. They were nervous. Jed behaved as if he was looking for the sheriff to help him and the sheriff had the look of a powerless man. Daniel noticed their behaviour and was lost in thought. 'Marshal, what do you want me to do with this gent?' the sheriff asked.

'Hmmm?' Daniel replied. 'Oh, lock him up – and those two cowboys over there. They are accomplices to the fact.'

Joe and Tom stood to attention. 'We had nothing to do with it,' Joe pleaded.

Once again, Daniel gave a sigh. 'Do I really have to spell things out?'

'I tell yer, Marshal, you're makin' a big mistake. We had nothing to do with it.'

Daniel noticed Murphy trading guns with Olga and his eyes opened wide. 'I cannot believe what I have just seen! Firstly you shoot a man stone dead with a normal scattergun, and now you have just exchanged it for something with more killing power than is necessary. Whilst I was in India I saw a gun much the same as that and it was used for killing elephants. What do you expect to do with that thing, shoot them both and take half the building as well?'

Hearing this, the cowboys raised their hands in submission. 'Don't let him shoot us, Sheriff. We'll come quietly.' Joe pointed to Murphy. 'Now just go real easy and don't put any pressure on that trigger. Tell him, Marshal!'

Daniel gave a loud tut and rolled his eyes. 'Now you have just seen a demonstration of my deputy's lack of self-control, so may I suggest you unbuckle your gun-belts slowly and kick them over here?' They both thought for a moment and looked at one another. 'If I were you I would not have any thoughts of drawing those pistols: my deputy's demonstration of his flagrant disregard of human life must be testimony enough, but seeing as there is a slight possibility you may decide to ignore his graphic warning, I will take this opportunity to move from the field of conflict and go and sit over there until this matter has been resolved one way or the other.'

Olga moved forward to stand shoulder to shoulder with Murphy. 'What'll it be, boys?' Murphy asked. 'Make one wrong move and you're dead meat.'

The cowboys undid their belts slowly and kicked them over. 'Wait one second, boys. How about you on the left throwin' me that peashooter you got in your breast holster? Real easy now; I got an itchy trigger finger.'

With great care, Lucky Joe reached inside his waistcoat and produced a Colt .38. 'It ain't loaded, Deputy, but you can have it all the same.' He placed it on the floor and kicked it over. 'That's it, we're clean.'

'And the knife in your boot,' Murphy said, 'or do you want to be Unlucky Joe?'

Joe pushed the knife across the floor as he was told.

Olga moved further forwards and picked up the knife and all three weapons as Murphy held them at gunpoint. 'I shoots zem anyway for trying to make you a fool?'

Daniel jumped up. 'My God! She is much worse than you. What a fine couple you make.' He waved an accusing finger at Murphy. 'I blame all this on you. Try to get her to exercise a little self control; these men are unarmed.'

'Zen give zem back zeir guns, zen I vill shoots them,' Olga said.

'No, I will not,' Daniel shouted. 'Sheriff, get these three to the safety of jail as soon as possible. I will sort things out here.'

The sheriff looked uneasy. 'Errr . . . come on, boys, let's have you now.'

The sheriff and the three prisoners left in the direction of the jail whilst Murphy, Daniel and Olga waited for the doctor and undertaker.

Murphy handed Olga her gun back. 'What in tarnation do you need a thing like this for?'

'I protect my man, zat is all,' she replied with a smile.

'Hey, Marshal,' Murphy began. 'Is he goin' to take them rascals to jail? I don't know if you reckon the way I do but that sheriff is in it up to his neck.'

'Of course I know that but there is very little else he can do. He can hardly pretend they got the better of him and made their getaway. Besides, all those men will be on the wanted list if they did and every bounty hunter will have a clean trail to follow. No, now that his little plan has gone wrong he is left to sort things out another way but that way will have to be decided by whomsoever is in charge and that man is the one we are after.'

'You know who zis man is?'

'That'll be Bannister – I'd stake my life on it,' Murphy replied.

'Zen I shoots him too.'

Daniel gave another exasperated sigh. 'Will you listen to yourselves? Is killing folk the solution to all your problems? All you think about is killing suspects, and this cannot continue ... and ... and ... and whilst we are sorting matters out, who invited Olga to join us?'

She smiled and gave Murphy a huge, suffocating hug. 'He is my big man and I looks out for him very well.'

'One thing I've got to say, Marshal: just then we could have done with as many guns as possible and you ain't no good at that if you ain't got no gun.'

'My dear man, I have never had the need to carry

a firearm and doubt very much I ever shall. My skills are quite obvious, as are yours, so shall we leave it to you to do the indiscriminate killing and me to do the complicated thinking?'

Murphy gave a grunt and shrugged his shoulders. 'I reckon so,' he said.

'Deputy, I take it you are not familiar with the game of chess?'

Murphy rubbed his chin. 'I ain't never heard of chess but I can play a mean hand at poker.'

'Quite. Well, the object of the game is to capture your opponent's king. In order to accomplish this one has to manoeuvre various pieces around the game board and small pieces of various values are almost unavoidably lost in the process. However, the game has begun and so far we are the first to draw blood, so to speak, and if Bannister is the king we wish to capture, we have played our pieces in accordance with his first move. That is to say, we take turns until the game is won. He had the first move and we had the second, so the next thing we have to do is wait until he makes the next move, and so on and so forth. Agreed?'

'You sure do talk funny.'

CHAPTER 9

The following morning Murphy was sitting in Katie's Eating House when Clarence and Claude came in through the door. As they spotted Murphy at his table they both curled their fingers up into tiny fists and clapped them together in boyish excitement before sitting down next to the deputy. Together they beamed with delight as they considered the events that had taken place the previous day.

'We heard what happened yesterday in the Golden Slipper and I can state on behalf of my dear brother Claude that we are very impressed indeed.'

Claude nodded his little head in agreement. 'Oh yes, very impressed indeed.'

Murphy grinned and pushed out his chest in pride. 'Guess I was pretty good when it comes to it. The way I dropped Red Flowers before he could shoot the marshal took a mighty piece of skill, I can tell you that for nothing.'

'Oh dear,' Clarence said. 'I'm afraid to say that did mar the events somewhat, because we are referring to the way Marshal Wheetman conducted himself. It was truly a masterpiece in detection – fingerprints, I believe?'

Murphy growled in protest. 'Now just wait a minute here. If'n it hadn't been for me, the fool marshal would have had his head blowed clean off. You two are just as crazy as he is.'

'Now, now, Mr Patterson,' Claude said. 'We certainly do appreciate your part in the events, but we both feel that in future you may consider wounding your victims rather than despatching them without a second thought.'

Clarence leaned closer to Murphy and spoke quietly. 'We feel it may be more productive to capture witnesses rather than blowing them in half before they have the chance to utter a word in their own defence.'

Murphy's face went red with rage as he rose to his full height of six feet four and, pointing a finger at them both, he hissed his reply. 'Now you two runts had better get this straight! There ain't no way I'm goin' to let anyone get the drop on me or the marshal, no matter what, and if'n I have to shoot in self-defence I ain't goin' to shoot other than to kill the mangy varmint who was tryin' to kill me in the first place. Are you two cottonin' on to what I'm talking about?'

Claude cleared his throat nervously. 'Ahem, we both fully understand, Mr Patterson, and you have our complete confidence.'

Murphy scowled at Clarence, who uttered his own

reply. 'Indeed, Mr Patterson,' he began. 'What my brother and I clearly fail to understand is the pressure you undergo and the split-second timing you require in order to fully anticipate the actions of a possible adversary. Isn't that so, brother?'

'Indeed it is,' Claude replied.

Murphy looked confused as he sat down again slowly. 'Does that mean I did good?'

'Indeed it does, Mr Patterson,' Clarence agreed. 'When we surrender our report we will make it clear you had little alternative but to shoot that poor man at close range – errr, with a scattergun – blowing off part of his chest and killing him almost instantly.'

Murphy smiled. 'Now that sounds right friendly to me gentlemen, and so as there's no ill feelin', I'll let you pay for my breakfast.' He sipped his coffee and then looked puzzled. 'Anyway, where was you two when all this stuff was goin' on?'

Claude looked nervously at Clarence. 'We were in a meeting when we heard the shots.'

Murphy grinned as he leaned forward and touched the side of Clarence's stiff white collar. 'Lipstick, if'n I'm not mistaken, and bright red lipstick at that.' He slapped his thigh and began to rock with laughter. 'You were at Rosie's Cathouse,' he declared loudly.

The twins begged him not to be so loud. 'Shhh, please,' Claude said.

Clarence leaned closer and spoke softly. 'If that were to be the case – and we are not saying it is – how could a little red mark on my brother's collar give

98

you such an impression that we, government agents, were to visit . . . how can we put it . . . a house of ill repute?'

Murphy's eyes grew wide with delight as he told them his secret. 'The marshal told me so.' The deputy looked cautiously from side to side to see if anyone was listening. 'I don't know if you've noticed the marshal writing in that little black book now and again?'

'Yes, we have,' they agreed.

'Well, he tells me he uses some sort of special handwriting which he learned in England. I think it's called backhand. . . . No, that's not it. Gunhand . . . no, that's not it either . . . Well, either way, he writes down all such things as what folk are wearin', doin', eatin' and anythin' else he thinks fit.'

'We don't quite follow you,' Clarence pointed out.

'If'n you let me finish, I'll tell you what I know,' Murphy growled. 'Now somehow he'd noticed little red marks on some folk's clothes and he wrote it all down in his little book, until one day he asked Mr Wong, who washes shirts and such like, what those marks were, and he told him it was lipstick.'

'Oh, come now,' Claude interrupted. 'How could he possibly understand Mr Wong?'

'I agree,' Clarence said. 'We take our laundry to Mr Wong and he hardly speaks a word of English – certainly not enough to talk about ladies' makeup.'

'No, but the marshal can speak Chinese,' Murphy explained, 'and Wong told him that it was lipstick, and every goddamned one the same at that: same colour and always on the collar of gents' duds.'

Claude reached to where his red mark should have been but Murphy explained where his was. 'Yours is on t'other side,' the deputy began to laugh again. 'Old Rosie must have marked yours so she could tell you two runts apart.'

'But how did she do this, and why?' Claude asked.

'Well, accordin' to the marshal, she gives every visitor a welcomin' hug and plants her bright red lips on every man's collar. She sort of brands 'em, like they were cattle or some such.'

'Oh, my,' Clarence said. 'This will never do.'

'Indeed,' Claude agreed.

Murphy grinned. 'Don't worry, boys, your secret is safe with me, which is just as well because the marshal is about to come and join us.'

The door opened and in its frame stood Daniel, who swiftly removed his fedora and stepped back politely in order to allow a large man and what appeared to be his large wife to enter the eating-house. 'Thank you, Marshal,' the man said as he held out his hand in friendship. 'The name's Gaffney, Walter Gaffney, and this is my wife, Elizabeth. I'm the mayor of this town.' Walter wore a grey suit with black velvet lapels, carefully trimmed with black buttons. His wife wore a grey dress with black satin finishing, almost matching his attire. They sat down quite near the door and beckoned the marshal to join them for breakfast.

Daniel smiled. 'That is very kind of you but I must join my friends over at the far table.' He gave a short bow and turned away, only to turn back even quicker and fix his eyes on Walter's collar.

Feeling uneasy, the mayor turned to look up at Daniel. 'What is it, Marshal? Something got your attention?'

'Why, yes, as you come to mention it,' the marshal replied. 'I couldn't help noticing that little red. . . .'

'Marshal!' The twins yelled in unison. 'We're over here!'

Daniel looked confused. 'I was just going to point out to the mayor that he has . . .'

Suddenly, both twins rushed forward and grabbed the marshal's arms. 'We must insist you join us straight away.' They smiled at Mr and Mrs Gaffney and hauled Daniel away. After they sat him down firmly they began to whisper in his ear. 'Those marks on his collar,' Claude began. 'It would not be a good idea to mention them in front of his wife.'

Daniel paused for thought. 'Oh, I see,' he said. 'I suppose that would be a little obtuse.'

Murphy narrowed his eyes. 'Whatever that means, I suppose it wouldn't be a good thing. You know, it sticks in my crawl when I think of that son of a gun. The mayor visitin' Rosie's Cathouse. . . . It's varmints like him that get all high and mighty and then take the time to send innocent folk like me to prison.'

'Innocent?' Claude said.

Clarence pointed his finger at his briefcase. 'We were at the courthouse during your trial and when all those charges were read out we could hardly believe our ears, I have them written down in here if you

101

wish me to remind you of them?'

Murphy shuffled awkwardly from side to side. 'Well, it ain't right, that's all. Maybe I have taken a few cattle in my time but that was only to repay monies owed to me.'

'And the bank robberies?' Claude said.

'Nobody ain't goin' to see their loved ones starve to death in the wintertime when there's plenty of money goin' spare in those bank vaults,' he nodded in the direction of the Gaffneys. 'It's folk like him that get rich and fat on the backs of poor honest men like me and it ain't right.' He tapped the table with his index finger. 'Where was he last night when I was upholding the law so that folk can sleep easy in their beds? Because of lawmen like me there's three men in that jail over yon'. What have you got to say about that?'

Daniel gave a cough. 'Well, now you come to mention it, there should have been four. How are we going to get enough evidence and information to establish who killed Sheriff Hayes when you go around like some crazed assassin who is paid purely on commission, the monetary value of which is established by some gruesome body count?'

'What in the name of hell is an assassin?' Murphy asked.

'A hired killer,' Clarence replied.

Murphy gritted his teeth, folded his arms and sat firm. 'I ain't sayin' any more; all you do is put me down,' he mumbled.

'Now come, come, Deputy,' Clarence said. 'Please

believe us when we say we have every confidence in your abilities and we do take your point about the marshal's safety being paramount.'

Claude did his best to change the subject and cool things down, so he turned towards Daniel and smiled. 'Marshal, although you come highly recommended, my brother and I know very little about you – your school or experience, for instance. We believe you spent some time in India?'

Daniel placed his cane on the table in front of him and positioned his hat on the vacant chair to his left. 'Well, there is very little to tell you. I was born in India but my parents sent to me to Whitewalls Boarding School in Surrey. It was there I met a boy called Sherlock who, like me, had an interest in detection. I remember we would set one another tasks based on deduction and investigation. There were always plenty of things going on: missing money, stolen watches, even identity fraud, and Sherlock and I would compete in order to solve any mystery.'

He gave a long smile followed by a sigh. 'Every now and then I would return to India, but I was really raised by my Aunt Sylvia and Uncle James. Uncle James worked in the Foreign Office and it was because of him my talents came to the attention of Her Majesty the Queen; well, that and the fact Sherlock and I managed to recover a priceless jewel that went missing at Whitewalls.'

'Aw, that don't make no sense,' Murphy interrupted. 'If'n it didn't have any price, what was the use of finding it? That don't make no sense.'

Daniel gave an audible tut. 'For your information; my ignoramus colleague, the term "priceless" does not mean without any value. It means its value is so high it is impossible to place a value upon it.'

Murphy scratched his head in thoughtful consideration. 'Does ignoramus mean good?'

Daniel nodded. 'It certainly does, and one may say your grasp of the English language is "priceless", but now, with your permission, I will endeavour to continue. As I was saying, Sherlock and I recovered the real Emerald Star, which was a diamond with a faint hew of an emerald. You see, it had been stolen and substituted by a fake, but we deduced its whereabouts and Her Majesty's law and order force reclaimed it, so to speak. As a direct result of this, when we became of age, Sherlock received a substantial sum of money and became a private detective, and I took the chance of working for Her Majesty in an investigative capacity, and the rest is history, as they say.'

'What colour was this so-called Emerald Star?' Murphy asked.

'It was an emerald-coloured diamond,' Claude pointed out.

'I heard what he said,' Murphy gasped. 'I just don't know what colour an emerald is.'

'Green,' Daniel explained.

'Ain't diamonds supposed to be like glass? I saw one once after Jack Shepherd robbed this fancy store in Santa Fe. Me and the boys were on our way to pick up five hundred head of beef and stopped off for a while, just to clear the dust from our craws and pick up some beans and stuff. We was sittin' watchin' a dance show when Jack came and sat at our table. Jack was one for the ladies and he saw one on the stage. She was dancing up a storm – kickin' her pretty little legs this way then that; I swear you could see all her underwear. Anyway, two days afore Jack had held up a stagecoach, so he was carryin' quite a wad of money and he decided to buy this little lady a weddin' ring even though he'd never said not a single word in jest to her. Before he could, he'd spent most of it buyin' everyone drinks and then lost the rest at poker. He was as drunk as a skunk and could hardly stand, but Jack decides to rob this here store right in the middle of town so he could give her a ring.

'Jack waited until it was quiet, then covered his face with his neckerchief and dropped his hat almost over his eyes. Inside the store he pulled his pistol and told the man behind the counter he wanted a special ring with a single diamond,' Murphy grinned, half-bit his lip and shook his head. 'Man – I can still see it shinin'. Like a star, it was. When Jack got back to the saloon he was grinning from ear to ear like a cat that had just got the cream, holdin' this ring high in the air for everyone to see. He sat down at a table near to the front and waited for his sweetheart to come back a-dancing but it wasn't long before a lawman came in with three deputies. I reckon the man at the store must have watched Jack staggerin' back to the saloon.'

Murphy leaned closer, almost speaking in confidence. 'You see, Jack was never the brightest of the bunch but when he was all liquored up he never did make any sense. Anyway, those lawmen strolled up to Jack all casual like and asked for the ring. They had him at gunpoint, but before things got out of hand someone shouted they had won all Jack's bullets not more'n an hour ago. I don't know how many lawmen Jack could see, maybe eight or nine, but Jack did his best to focus on one of 'em. He tried to pull his pistol but dropped it then and there, right at their feet. Old Jack was scrabblin' about on the floor when he started to laugh so loud he fell asleep right where he was.

'They carried him out, put him in jail and returned the ring to the store. The following day he was released and told never to come back again.'

'Oh, my,' Clarence said. 'And did he leave?'

'He had a mind not to and started cussin' and stompin' his feet, so those lawmen escorted him to his horse where, unlucky for Jack, they found the payroll bag from the stage he'd robbed three days earlier. You see, Jack thought it would make a mighty fine feedbag so he kept it. From what I heard he got two years.'

Daniel gave a sigh. 'And what was the purpose of that riveting story?'

'Well, it goes to show that those lawmen let Jack go because he was drunk and not of fit mind; after all, no one got hurt.'

Daniel looked at Murphy with withering eyes. 'Yes,

but he was guilty of robbing the stage.'

'That ain't nothin' to do with it,' Murphy protested. 'It's men like that mayor over yon' who do one thing and mean another . . . Hey, Marshal, what you writin'?'

'I am merely making a few notes,' Daniel said as he showed Murphy his book quickly.

'Now maybe I ain't too good at readin' an all, but that don't look like any words to me.'

'May we take a look, Marshal?' Claude asked.

Daniel passed them his notebook. 'My, my,' Clarence said. 'I take it this is some kind of short-hand?'

'Yes, it is our very own. Sherlock and I invented it so that nobody could read our notes.'

Murphy grabbed the book off them and began to blush. 'Now I know you're pullin' my pecker,' he said. 'This here squiggle looks like a lady's titty, and so does this, and this one looks like a lady's tushtush.'

Daniel carefully took his notebook back and placed it in his pocket. 'I can assure you it is fine and proper and is merely a way of recording events in a quick and easy manner. As for you, you are obviously sex mad.'

'Whatever you say, Marshal, but you sure are a dark horse.'

'Oh, never mind.' Suddenly Daniel noticed the silhouette of a man checking his revolver outside the front of the eating-house and beckoned to Murphy, who immediately flipped the leather trigger loop off his Colt. Before the door could open, Daniel and the

107

twins moved quickly to a table on the left-hand side and between them they waited for the next move.

Slowly and deliberately, the door swung open and in walked a thin man dressed like a cowboy but with his holster low on his right leg. His Colt rested high in the holster so the whole of the trigger guard was visible. His steel grey eyes surveyed the room carefully until he saw Murphy. 'You the deputy?' he asked.

'Reckon I am,' Murphy replied slowly.

'Ain't nothing personal,' he said with menace. 'Just business.'

'I know,' Murphy replied.

'There's innocent folk here, shall we sort this thing out in the street?'

'Suits me,' Murphy said as he rose from his seat carefully.

The man moved backwards towards the door slowly when all of a sudden his Colt was lifted from its holster and slid neatly into the hands of Marshal Wheetman. Murphy pulled his gun and challenged the man to make one wrong move. 'Stranger, if'n you know what's good for ya, I'd put my hands high in the air.'

The gunman did as Murphy suggested then looked at the marshal, who was holding his gun. 'That ain't fair!' he argued. 'He took away my pistol with that sword thing.'

Daniel handed the stranger's gun to Murphy then triumphantly returned his sword into its walking cane scabbard.

Murphy grinned. 'I've wondered why you carry that stick with you when you ain't got no gammy leg.'

'It has its uses,' the marshal replied casually as he turned his attention to the stranger. 'Now, sir, may I ask you to sit down so we may have a little chat?' He pulled a chair out and the stranger sat down whilst Murphy kept his gun carefully trained at the man's chest. 'Before we continue, I must point out how I find it extremely difficult to get some of you to understand there are more ways to settle a disagreement other than the use of gratuitous violence. Your propensity for a "shoot first ask questions later" policy is positively mind-boggling.'

The stranger looked puzzled. 'You sure do talk funny,' he said.

'Don't he?' Murphy drawled.

'Now, sir,' the marshal began. 'What disagreement do you have with my deputy?'

'I ain't got no disagreement, I ain't never seen him before. I was told he was in here and what he looks like by some fella in the street; a preacher, he said.'

'Then am I to assume you are an assassin?'

Murphy grinned as he looked at the stranger. 'You ain't got no idea what an assassin is, don't ya? Well, I've heard that one before: an assassin is someone who kills folk and such?'

'I ain't sayin' nothing – and you didn't have call to cheat the way you did. Why, usin' that sword in a gun-fight ain't called for. It ain't right.'

Daniel shook his head in disbelief. 'Once again, I am flabbergasted. If I had not intervened in your

109

ridiculous habits of cavorting in a most juvenile manner, it is almost a certainty that one or both of you would be lying out there on the floor right now in a pool of blood.' He gave a large sigh. 'Oh dear, we may as well take him to the jail and have a word with him later.'

'"Take him to jail"? Now *that* I understand,' the stranger said.

'Wait for us,' the twins shouted as they came from under the table.

As they left for the jail, those in the eating-house broke out with applause.

CHAPTER 10

Murphy, the stranger and Daniel stood outside the jailhouse whilst the twins peered through the dirty windows. 'We've tried the locks and we can't see anyone, Marshal,' Claude explained. 'The sheriff must be out.'

'How very convenient,' the marshal replied as he took a peculiar shaped key from his pocket. He pushed it into the lock and after several twists and wriggles the door bolt shot and the door swung open. 'That you, Sheriff?' came a voice from the cells in the back. 'We sure hope you bought us that whiskey you promised. Anything from Bannister?'

'Not anything you would like to hear,' the marshal replied.

'Marshal!' came the unmistakable voice of Jed Walsh. 'I guess the sheriff is with you?'

'He most certainly is not, but fortunately he left the door open. However, have no fear, gentlemen. We will lock it soundly on our way out; that is, as soon as we have managed to deposit another customer for

111

an unknown period of temporary incarceration in this rather dismal place.'

The stranger turned to Murphy. 'He ain't changed his mind, has he? Only he sure do talk funny.'

'Stranger,' he replied with a smile, 'if'n we hadn't got off to a bad start I reckon we could have become good friends.'

The twins searched the sheriff's desk, found the cell keys and gave them a triumphant rattle to announce their discovery. 'Here they are, Marshal,' Clarence cried.

Murphy pushed his gun between the stranger's shoulders. 'You go first,' he growled. 'And keep those hands where I can see 'em.'

The stranger moved forwards slowly until he could see the three men in the cells. 'Carver!' Jed shouted.

'Shut your big mouth,' Carver snapped back.

'Moses Carver!' Murphy shouted. 'He done killed over ten men.'

'How was you taken, Carver?' Ben asked. 'Bet it took a mighty big posse?'

'Actually, I disarmed Mr Carver myself,' the marshal explained.

'You? Ben gasped. 'You ain't even got no gun.'

''T'ain't fair. He done snook up on me like some Injun and used a sword to take away my gun. He keeps it in that fancy stick of his. I tell ya, boys, he don't play fair.'

'Yes, Marshal,' Ben pointed out. 'That ain't fair.'

Daniel gave a sigh. 'Am I to take it there is some sworn code of conduct one has to adhere to in order to satisfy the traditions of the west? Maybe there is a secret brotherhood that meets every Thursday in Lent to discuss the inclusion of a new modus operandi for every man and boy who rides the range. But as far as I am aware, there is no such code and there never will be, so if you would be so kind, Mr Carver, as to join Mr Ballard in his cell, I would most grateful.'

Carver went into the cell and Clarence locked the cage door. 'Oh my, Claude,' he said. 'My heart is positively pounding at the thought of me being the man who locked up Moses Carver.'

Carver made a grab through the bars at Clarence but missed by an inch. 'Why, you son of a bitch, I'll get you: you see if I don't.'

Clarence stood back, shook his little fist and hissed at Carver. 'Why, you . . . you very naughty man, you.'

Claude stepped up. 'And that goes for me too,' he added.

Carver paced around the cell grumbling then pointed to Daniel. 'I tells ya, what he did wasn't fair. We had the makin's of a good honest gunfight, man-to-man, and he cheated.'

'He did not,' Murphy argued.

'He did too,' Carver insisted.

'Did not,' Murphy shouted.

'Did too,' Carver shouted back.

The marshal covered his ears in disbelief. 'Children, children!' he shouted. 'It is like working in a kindergarten for the over-privileged with your "did not" and "did too". May I remind you we are dealing with a very serious matter?'

'Oh indeed,' Claude agreed. 'Very serious indeed.'

'Oh yes, very serious,' Clarence added.

All four of them heard the office door open and listened as footsteps came in their general direction. Murphy pointed his Colt, ready for action.

'Who's there?' The sheriff's voice rang out.

Tom Williams grabbed the bars and lifted himself up slightly in an effort to see well. 'It's the marshal, his deputy and two half-pints. They gone and took Moses Carver,' he shouted. 'He's locked up with Lucky Joe.'

The sheriff came into view. 'On what charge?' he asked.

Daniel smiled, shrugged his shoulders and pushed Murphy's pistol out of harm's way gently. 'Take your pick,' he began. 'Disturbing the peace, menacing behaviour, illegal duelling, action likely to cause harm, provocation, illegal use of a firearm or even attempted manslaughter, I could think of many more, but those should be sufficient for now.'

The sheriff removed his hat and scratched his head. 'That gives me four prisoners to take care of. How come they can't get out on bail?'

Daniel frowned as he pointed at Murphy to holster his gun. 'I must apologise for the extra zeal my deputy demonstrates when it comes to using one of his ubiquitous firearms to solve the smallest problem.'

Murphy grinned as he put his gun away. 'Now there's shows what you know,' he said. 'This here's a Colt and not an unbix . . . whatever, so haw-haw, Mr

114

Know-It-All: this time you got it wrong.'

'He did, too,' Carver laughed. 'And him so high and mighty.'

'Philistines,' the marshal muttered as he looked at the sheriff. 'Now, as I was about to say, all of these men will be given the correct and proper treatment as is required by law. However, there remains the probability they are wanted for other crimes committed in the past, so I thoroughly recommend their incarceration to be as long as possible in order for sufficient enquiries to take place to ascertain if that possibility is a fact or not.' He replaced his fedora and gave the brim a gentle tap with his cane. 'They may be wanted for bigger crimes, possibly crimes which will see them hanged. Who knows?'

Lucky Joe grabbed the bars and gave them a good shake. 'You got to get me out, Sheriff – you and Bannister never said nothin' about no hangin'.'

Murphy pulled his gun and narrowed his eyes at the sheriff. 'Don't make any sudden moves; just do as I say,' he demanded.

The marshal gave a tut. 'Here we go again,' he sighed. 'Sheriff, I can see by your bedazzled expression you are somewhat amazed to find yourself at gunpoint in your own office, but my deputy does have rather a good point. At least for the next few minutes, I would thoroughly recommend you do everything he asks.'

Murphy pushed his pistol forwards. 'Now unbuckle that holster real slow and drop it to the floor.' The sheriff did as he was told. 'Now, move over

115

to the cage bars so as we can see yer better.'

'For once I feel I may have to congratulate you, Deputy,' Daniel said. 'That reference to Bannister is rather incriminating.'

'I didn't tell him anythin', Sheriff,' Lucky Joe shouted. 'They know nothin' at all, and if they did they couldn't prove a thing.'

'Once again, I must make my point of it being rather like working in a kindergarten,' Daniel said in disbelief. 'I somehow think if I gave you all sufficient rope you would all hang yourselves.'

'I ain't done nothin', Marshal.' Carver shouted. 'I don't know nothin' about what they're sayin'.'

'Shall you choose which cell, Sheriff, or shall I choose it?' Murphy drawled.

Clarence spoke up in excitement. 'Oh, this is very exciting, may I choose?' he asked. 'And may I be the one to lock him up?'

'Certainly not; it has to be my turn,' Claude pointed to Carver. 'You locked that ruffian up.'

Clarence gave it a moment's thought. 'You are completely right, my dear brother. After all, it is not every day we get to lock villains up.'

'You are quite correct: not every day. In fact, we have never locked up any villains in our lives.'

Claude took the keys, unlocked the door and beckoned the sheriff to enter, Claude slammed the door closed behind him and turned the key. 'My goodness, that does feel rather satisfying, I must admit,' he said.

The sheriff sat down on the bed and grinned. 'You

116

boys don't have no idea what you're doin'. You can't keep us here for long, Marshal. Firstly, you ain't got no good reason to lock me up just because that loud-mouth blabbed, and secondly – well. . . . Well, I'll think of something.'

Daniel took a long calm look at the men in the cells. 'Sheriff, no doubt you are correct,' he began. 'However, as you have already witnessed my deputy's reaction to similar remarks made yesterday in the Golden Shoe, remarks that resulted in the death of Mr Flowers, I feel it my duty to detain you for your own safety.' He turned to walk away. 'In the mean-time, I shall leave my deputy to keep a safe watch on you all.'

Murphy grinned. 'Hey, Marshal, for once I got myself a jail which I can come and go whenever I wants to.'

'And I vill be viz him,' came Olga's voice as she stood filling the doorway with her massive, heavily armed frame. 'Who is first to be shot?' she said as she slammed her heavy-gauge shotgun closed. Her eyes scanned those in the cells until she closed in on Lucky Joe. 'Hmmm, he has eyes too close. I think him first.'

Joe threw his hands high in the air. 'Marshal!' he shouted. 'She's crazy, Marshal.'

Olga focused her steel blue eyes at Joe who wore a nervous smile. 'Beggin' your pardon, ma'am. No offence but I ain't responsible for what I say some-time.'

'You say me crazy,' she snapped back.

'I . . . I . . . I didn't mean nothin',' he stammered. 'I say that about lots for folk, don't I boys?'

Not knowing quite what to do, the rest gave a reluctant, half-hearted nod in agreement until Daniel thankfully intervened. 'Miss Olga,' he began. 'These fellows are finding it very hard to placate you. I must admit their task is Herculean considering your rather pragmatic attitude when it comes to dealing with anyone who is unfortunate to earn your displeasure, but may I ask if you would be so kind as to not shoot anyone unless one of our lives is in jeopardy?' He tilted his hat. 'Or your own life, I may add.'

Murphy gave a cough. 'Olga, what I think he means is don't shoot any of 'em unless they gets on your craw,' he said out loud.

'I most certainly do not,' the marshal protested. 'Getting on someone's craw, as you put it, can never be a good reason to shoot a fellow human being; no matter how annoying they may be, I am talking about restraint from killing.'

'I gets ya, Marshal,' he said as he pointed to Olga's gun. 'Hey, Olga, don't use that thing unless as I tell ya first.'

She looked puzzled, smiled and then lowered her gun. 'I do as my man says.'

'Eureka!' the marshal said with relief. 'Now, I take it I can leave these men in your safe custody, Deputy?'

Murphy gave a slight nod, left the cells, and walked into the office slowly. He rubbed his chin as he sat at the sheriff's desk then, rummaging through the drawers, he found a small box of cigars. 'OK to help myself to a cigar, Sheriff?' he shouted.

'Be my guest,' the sheriff replied begrudgingly.

Murphy put his feet up and placed a satisfying cigar to his lips, but before he could light it, it was snatched by Olga, who began to smoke it swiftly. 'Ahhh, zes are goot,' she said.

As he was about to leave, the marshal saw the gun rack on the wall. 'Ah, this is quite interesting,' he said as he touched one of the two rifles. 'If I am not mistaken, this is a Remington rolling block rifle?'

Murphy stood up, walked over and took it down. 'Yep, it sure is. I had one a few years ago. They are mighty reliable, but only a single shot.'

'I noticed the sheriff has a Remington revolver,' Daniel pointed out.

Murphy picked it up. 'He sure has – I prefer my Colt though.'

'Quite so, but the Remington has a slightly longer range; not by very many feet – possibly ten or so – but it can outshoot a Colt.'

Murphy rubbed his chin. 'How come you know so much about guns? I mean, it ain't like you carry one.'

'You are quite correct, Deputy, but in my line of work it pays dividends to always be aware of things you may not be familiar with, such as firearms.'

Murphy put the rifle back, sat down again and lit a cigar. 'You can leave everything to me, Marshal,' he groaned as he put his feet up.

'And me also,' Olga added.

'And us,' the twins spoke up. 'We will stay here and

help Mr Patterson, and of course this young lady.'

Daniel left, the twins sat down next to the stove and Olga stood watching the men in the cells, keeping her large-bore scattergun close by her side.

Murphy looked at Claude and furrowed his brow. 'Either of you two runts know why he's here instead of a proper marshal?'

The twins looked at each other and grinned. 'Indeed we do,' Clarence replied. 'As you are aware, President Hayes' nephew was murdered in Crows Creek, but that is only the tip of the iceberg, so to speak.'

Claude clapped his little hands together in excitement and bounced about in his chair. 'Oh, very good, my brother. Iceberg . . . I do rather like that.'

Clarence blushed. 'I do think it was rather clever, now you come to mention it, but I shall continue with my account of events in a more sombre manner from now on. You see, the iceberg refers to a ship, a ship that was on an Arctic exploration some years ago. When this ship became icebound the crew abandoned it, and after the spring thaw came it drifted into the open sea where it was recovered by our navy.'

Murphy took a long draw and rolled the smoke over his tongue. 'I don't get where you two are goin' with this story, so gets to the point.'

'I shall continue, if that is alright with you, Clarence?'

'Indubitably, my dear brother.'

'Well, this ship was called HMS *Resolute* and was taken to the Brooklyn Navy Yard where it was fully restored at the cost of the US government. Later, it was sailed back to England and presented to Queen Victoria as a gift. She was so impressed that she never forgot our country's wonderful gesture. After the ship had finished its commission she ordered it to be dismantled, and the oak from her was made into a wonderful desk, which she sent to President Hayes as a thank you. Now, since the unfortunate episode with President Lincoln, President Hayes has restored faith in the American presidency: possibly because of his stand on human rights, but more likely his stand on law and order. It was President Hayes who asked Her Majesty to help by furnishing him with a good detective, one who is beyond bribery, one who is beyond the reach of certain parties, one who has no reason but to act in a just and honourable way . . . and thus you have it: Daniel Wheetman.'

Clarence clapped his little hands together. 'A very good tale, dear brother, very well recorded indeed.'

Murphy grinned and deliberately asked the twins a question out loud. 'Hey boys, which one of those varmints in them there cells do ya think shot Sheriff Hayes?'

Claude thought for a while. 'Mr Carver does have a reputation for killing.'

'I ain't never shot anyone other than in a fair fight,' Carver shouted. 'I ain't never shot anyone in the back and for that matter I ain't shot anyone with my rifle, I've only shot folk with my handgun, face to face, man to man. I ain't no dirty low-down bush-whacker and that's a fact.'

121

'That a fact? You damn well came to try and gun me down,' Murphy replied, 'and we ain't never met.'

Olga pointed her four-gauge at Carver and cocked the hammer. 'Zis is true?' she asked. 'You came to kill my big man?'

'Now don't go pullin' that trigger, Olga: you know what the marshal said.'

Olga's snake eyes peered at Carver. 'Olga does as her man tells her and zis is wery good news for you, but next time I shoots you on sight, right between zose eyes.'

Murphy began to laugh. 'Olga, I do declare, if'n you hit him right between his eyes with that thing they'd be pickin' up what's left of 'em in New Mexico. Now just ease up and gently put the hammer back so as we can all relax and enjoy a cigar at the sheriff's expense.'

CHAPTER 11

After locking Carver and the sheriff in the jail, Daniel went to see the undertaker Jack Stoops. Stoops had a small black funeral parlour at the far end of town. Nobody knew for certain why he had it trimmed with pink and yellow ribbons. Some said it was for a cheerful effect, others said it was his favourite colours, but the truth of the matter was that he never gave the same explanation twice.

Stoops' thin grey face always had a sombre expression, so much so that some of his clients looked more alive than he did, especially after Stoops had plied his superior embalming skills to the faces of those deceased who had received his 'gold service treatment'.

However, there were those poor unfortunates who died penniless and the best Stoops would do for them was to plant them firmly in the corner of the cemetery with nothing but a pile of dust and stones to tell they were ever there. Stoops was a businessman, but there was something more: he loved death.

Daniel entered Stoops' dimly lit parlour to the sound of a small bell hanging from the door jam. He removed his hat and waited for Stoops. After a few moments the marshal heard the creaking of old leather shoes getting closer until Stoops appeared through a red and blue beaded blind. 'I take it you do not come to enquire about a service?' he asked in his ghostlike voice.

'My name is Marshal Wheetman,' Daniel began, 'but judging by your expression you already know that.'

Stoops closed his eyes, narrowed his mouth and gave a slow mechanical nod.

'I take it you prepared Sheriff Hayes for internment?' Daniel asked.

Once again Stoops gave a grave nod.

'I wonder if you would be so kind as tell me all you could ascertain from the state of the sheriff when he arrived here.'

Stoops beckoned Daniel to follow him into the back room. Next he led him to a large, black leather-bound book, which he opened at the page labelled 'Hayes'.

Daniel turned the book and began to read Stoops' entries. 'My word, you do keep very good records. It says here a single bullet entry wound in his back and a larger exit wound in his chest, cutting his vena cava almost in half. I take it the bullet was never located?'

Stoops shrugged his shoulders in dismay. 'Finding the bullet, my dear sir, is not my job,' he whispered.

'And yes, the vena cava had been shattered by the bullet.'

'But I see you noted the exact location of where the sheriff fell, and with such a wound I am certain death would have been almost immediate. Besides, here you noted the blood on the floor that proves he dropped where he was shot.'

'You are correct: death would have been instantaneous and the pool of blood confirms this.'

'And from your excellent records I see you made a calculated guess as to the angle the bullet passed through the sheriff's chest.'

'Once again, Marshal, you are correct. I find death and murder to be quite fascinating.'

'Did the sheriff appear to have drawn his pistol, or did he carry a second firearm such as a rifle?'

'No, he had not drawn his pistol and he was not carrying a second firearm.'

'May I borrow these notes so I can visit the exact place where he was shot?'

'You may not. However, I will accompany you to the spot.'

Stoops glided towards the front door, picked up his top hat gracefully, placed it under his arm and stepped back so Daniel could leave first. 'After you, Marshal,' he said with a grim smile.

Together they walked in slow silence until they reached a spot between the general store and the blacksmith's forge. Stoops pointed to the ground. 'Right here,' he said.

Daniel stood on the very spot and took bearings in

all directions. 'How was he laying?'

'Head in that direction, and his feet were here,' Stoops replied.

The marshal looked behind them. 'So the shot would have come from that direction?'

Stoops turned. 'Yes,' he began, 'from the direction of the livery stable or the barbershop. They are both in the line of fire.'

'Could it have come from the roof of the livery stable?'

'Indeed not: the angle of the bullet showed no elevated entry. It was fired from shoulder height or thereabouts.'

Daniel shook the undertaker's hand, headed back towards the jail, stopped, turned, doffed his hat and smiled. 'Thank you sir, you have been very helpful,' he said.

The marshal arrived at the jail and stood in front of Murphy in triumph. 'At last we have some decent evidence to go on.' Excited as an expectant father, he pointed to the twins. 'You two, come with us. Oh, and Deputy, bring that rifle.'

'I vill vate here and shoot zem ifs zey moves,' Olga added.

'What?' the marshal said as he tried to hurry things forwards. 'Oh, very well, I don't have the time to argue – but do try to wound them rather than litter the place up with a mountain of dead bodies.'

'Marshal, you can't do that,' Lucky Joe shouted. 'She's, errr, I mean . . . Oh never mind, Marshal, we'll be good.'

As all four reached the spot where Sheriff Hayes was shot, he told them the plan. 'This is where Hayes was found having been shot in the back from somewhere over there. We are going to reconstruct the events, which took place after dark last year. Firstly, I want you to lie down on the floor as if you were dead.'

'Oh my, I don't think that is a very good idea, Marshal,' Claude said. 'Why, to lie on the floor where a man died is just not right.'

'I'll do it, Marshal,' the blacksmith shouted. 'Henry Copeland's the name.' Copeland was a middle aged, heavily set man who wore a smile like none other: it was halfway between vacant and ecstatic and it fitted well between his very long ginger sideburns.

'Bravo!' the marshal replied, as he instructed Henry where and how to lie on the floor. 'Now this is how the sheriff's body was found, so we can deduce he was shot from over there.'

Murphy looked behind. 'That'll be the livery stable or the barbershop, Marshal.'

'Quite, but I can rule out the barbershop.'

'How the hell can you do that?' Murphy growled.

'Quite easily, because in front of the livery stable there are two water barrels, four thick wooden pillars and an assortment of wagons and other such paraphernalia behind which an assassin could easily conceal themselves. In addition it has an overhanging roof, which would form a handy shadow should the moon be bright. In contrast, the barbershop offers nothing but trouble: large windows that reflect the slightest shadow, it is painted white and, due to there being very little necessity in the walkway having to take or sustain a heavy load, we can assume it creaks. No, gentlemen, the livery stable it was.'

'Can I get up now, Marshal?'

'Of course you can, but may I ask another slight favour?'

'Go ahead, Marshal.'

'Just stand there whilst my deputy re-enacts the shooting.'

'Sure thing, Marshal,' Henry pulled up his britches with pride. 'Not often I get the chance to join a team of lawmen. Bet I don't get a badge?'

Daniel told Murphy to semi-conceal himself in front of the livery stable and take aim at Henry's heart. 'Now!' Daniel shouted. 'Cry out like you have just fired a fatal shot, and after you do, stay in that position until I say you can move.'

'What noise do I use?'

'"Bang!" will suffice.'

'Aw, shucks, Marshal, I'll just look plum stupid. Do I have to shout "bang"?'

'Bang is a perfect onomatopoeia. Everybody understands bang.'

'There you go again with your fancy words. You tryin' to make me look more stupid than I do. Holdin' this rifle and shoutin' "bang"? Can't I just fire one into the air?'

'Indeed not – just point the rifle at this gentle-man's heart and shout "bang!"'

Like a naughty schoolboy, Murphy lowered his head and shuffled his feet before doing as he was told. 'Bang!' he shouted, as two passing ladies began to giggle and take his attention.

Daniel eye's widened as he pointed an accusing finger at Murphy. 'You have moved. I told you not to move.'

'Well, that's because I just can't shout "bang!" with a rifle up agen my face.'

'What! Oh, very well, make some other noise, then.'

'What about a whistle, Marshal? I can whistle whilst I'm shootin'.'

'If that suits you better, go ahead, but after you have whistled, stay where you are. Do not move a muscle.'

'Do I stay here, Marshal?' Henry asked.

'You do indeed, but when you hear my deputy whistle, drop to the floor like you have just been shot.'

Daniel gave Murphy the signal and the deputy let out an ear-piercing whistle. However, Henry remained bolt upright whilst wearing his best smile. Daniel closed in on Henry. 'Mr Copeland?' he asked.

'Yes, Marshal?' Copeland replied.

'Did you not hear the signal?' the marshal asked.

'What signal?'

'My deputy gave out a whistle.'

'Oh, I guess I can't hear a whistle cause of the way I've been hitting them steel bars and such all my life, Marshal, but I can hear a bang.'

'This I do not believe,' Daniel muttered under his breath. 'Mr Copeland, did you hear when my deputy shouted "bang"?'

'Sure did, Marshal; good and deep his voice is, like a mule at suppertime. It's high notes I can't rightly hear.'

Daniel looked at the twins. 'Would one of you gentlemen mind going and standing next to the deputy and shouting "bang" at my signal?'

'I'm on my way,' Clarence said as he ran over to Murphy.

'Now,' Daniel shouted. 'When I drop my hand, you shout "bang", then my deputy will pretend to shoot Mr Copeland and when Mr Copeland hears the bang he will drop to the floor like he has been shot. Gentlemen, are you ready?' Daniel raised his hand and dropped it towards the floor swiftly.

In a high-pitched voice Clarence shouted 'bang!' as loud as he could, but Henry didn't flinch.

Daniel thought for a while, then stood in front of Henry, stared into his eyes and asked patiently, 'Mr Copeland, I take it you failed to hear that bang?'

'To be honest, Marshal, I didn't hear anything.'

'Deputy!' Daniel shouted tersely. 'Would you kindly pass Claude, or could it be Clarence, a stick or some such other device so he can rap on one of those barrels?' Murphy did as he was told and Clarence struck the barrel hard. 'Now, Mr Copeland, did you hear that?'

'Loud and clear, Marshal,' he grinned with pride.

'Very good. The next time you hear that sound,

drop to the floor like you had just been shot.' Daniel told everyone to take position and dropped his hand again. This time the blacksmith heard the sound, gave out a painful groan, clutched his chest, fell to the ground, rolled over four times and began crawling forwards on his hands and knees in the general direction of the doctors.

Daniel closed his eyes and offered a small prayer for help.

Murphy burst out laughing. 'Shall I shoot him again, Marshal? Looks like I only winged him. Or shall I call Olga to bring that scattergun of hers?'

'Henry!' the marshal shouted. 'You are not supposed to move other than to fall on the spot.' He pointed to the ground. 'This spot here, the very same spot I asked you to lie down in.'

Copeland got up, dusted himself down indignantly and strolled back to the spot. 'Just as you say, Marshal, only I was tryin' to put some realism into the whole thing.'

Daniel gave a sigh. 'Gentlemen, please be reminded we are not trying to emulate the great works of Shakespeare but merely trying to establish where the bullet went after it passed through the sheriff's chest. If we can try again I would be very grateful, and perhaps sometime in the very near future we will be able to move on and Henry go back to his occupation of hitting hot pieces of metal.' He straightened his fedora, held his cane high and swished it towards the ground.

Clarence hit the barrel, Henry dropped to the

ground and Murphy continued to aim.

'That's it!' he exclaimed. 'Now, Deputy, what are you aiming at?'

'The escape route from Rosie's Cathouse,' Murphy replied.

'You mean the staircase?'

'Sure do.'

'Quick, gentlemen, we must find where that bullet is. Search every inch, leave nothing to chance.' He rushed over to the side of the cathouse. 'Somewhere here we shall find the bullet that killed Sheriff Hayes.'

'That ain't no good, Marshal,' Murphy insisted.

'Oh no, Deputy, I beg to differ. It will tell us a great deal.'

The five of them searched until Claude found what they were looking for, slightly embedded in the side of one of the stair runs. 'I've found it, Marshal.' He shouted.

'Well done, Claude,' Clarence said.

Daniel used Murphy's best knife to winkle the bullet out carefully.

'I've told ya so, Marshal, that ain't goin' to tell you anything,' Murphy grumbled.

The marshal held it in his fingers and smiled at Murphy. 'Oh, what a tangled web we weave, when once we practise to deceive.'

'You sure do talk funny.'

CHAPTER 12

Daniel took the recovered bullet to his room and did a full study whilst the others returned to the jail so that Olga could resume her new job at Katie's Eating House. It was not that Olga was perfect for the job or she was the only applicant. Her employment was based simply on the fact Katie could not say no to her – nobody could.

For reasons best known to him, Henry Copeland had decided he was a member of the team and wherever they went he took with him his beaming smile.

It dawned on the twins that since the sheriff was in jail there was nobody there to provide the prisoners with food, so they took the task in hand.

Claude decided it was his duty to make certain the prisoners received a meal to their likings so he had his writing pad ready as Clarence took their orders. 'Now, gentlemen, what would each of you wish by way of food?' he said dutifully.

'Ben and me want stew,' Tom ordered.

'Two stews,' Clarence said as Claude wrote it down.

'Stew for me as well,' Lucky Joe added.

'That's three stews – and for you, Sheriff?'

'Steak and potatoes,' he replied.

'And for you, Mr Carver?'

'I'll have the same.'

'Oh my – does that mean the same as those boys or the same as the sheriff?'

'Steak and potatoes,' Carver snapped back.

'Very well,' Clarence said. 'My brother and I will take your order over to the eating house and upon our return we trust everything *will* be in order.'

Claude clapped his hands together in excitement. 'Oh, very good, dear brother; very droll.'

As they left, they passed Daniel in the doorway. 'Where are you two going?' he questioned. 'I need you both for a scientific experiment.'

'We are going to get some food for the prisoners,' Clarence replied.

'Food? Oh yes, I suppose we do have to feed them. Well, come back as soon as you can: we have work to do.'

Claude looked concerned. 'Errr . . . we don't like to have to tell you, Marshal, but we do not work for you.'

'Indeed,' Clarence added, but his words fell on deaf ears, as Daniel was lost in his work.

'Hmmm? Yes, very good. Now go and return as soon as possible.' The marshal waved one hand in dismissal of the twins, and with the other showed the spent bullet to Murphy as he leaned close to whisper. 'This could not be better, Deputy: .42 calibre and, unless I am very much mistaken, it was shot from a Remington rolling block rifle like the one over there.'

'But you don't know that,' Murphy whispered back.

'Not at the moment, but all will be revealed after our little experiment.'

'What in tarnation are you blabbin' about, Marshal?'

'We are going to fire a bullet from this rifle through a side of beef and into some soft wood, then we are going to examine the marks the barrel has left on the bullet and compare it with those made on the bullet that killed Sheriff Hayes.'

'Have you gone mad?'

'Not in the least; you see, those weapons whose barrels are rifled scratch every bullet in their own unique way and identically. Just as fingerprints are unique, so are barrel marks.'

'You mean to say you can tell which gun fired what bullet?'

'Without a shadow of doubt, I can, but let us see if we can establish exactly who owns the Remington rifle before we begin.' The marshal took both rifles into the cells and showed them to Sheriff Stoppard. 'I see you keep your rifles clean,' he said.

'And my pistol too,' he replied.

'This Remington, have you had it long?' Daniel asked.

'First rifle I ever had.'

'Yes, I gather they are rather reliable. Quite tough,

you may say?'

'She ain't never let me down.'

'Not that you are in a position to argue, but good manners force me to ask if we may try it out?'

'Be my guest. There are some cartridges in my desk.'

'Oh, I only require one, Sheriff – just the one.'

'You'll find she's bang-on accurate.'

Daniel smiled and doffed his hat before returning to the office and replacing the rifle on the wall. 'There are some cartridges in one of the desk drawers. If you would bring one with you over to the butcher's then I would be most grateful, along with, of course, the rifle in question.'

Murphy rose to his feet, stretched, scratched, shook his head and began to search for the cartridges. 'This I must see,' he mumbled.

Because of the role-play incident earlier, some of the townsfolk who had bore witness to the pretend shooting had gathered into a discussion group and they were waiting eagerly for the next episode. When Daniel and Henry came out of the jail, Stumpy, the town drunk, led a small procession after them. 'Henry!' he shouted. 'What's you going to do next?'

Henry looked back as they hurried onwards. 'Not got time right now, Stumpy; this is official business.'

Stumpy took a swig from his bottle, wobbled to his left and fixed Daniel with both bloodshot eyes. 'Marshal,' he shouted. 'It ain't fair. I wanna be a deputy too.'

When Daniel and Henry burst into the butcher's

store, he was cutting up a large shank. 'Abe, this here is the marshal, and he's got this crazy plan you just got to see.'

'Plan, you say?' Abe replied.

'He sure has. Did you see me earlier? I was right in the thick of it helping the marshal with his investigation. I tells ya, he sure is a clever one.'

Abe cleaned his hands on his apron. 'What exactly can I do for yer, Marshal?'

'I need to hire a side of beef,' Daniel explained.

Abe rubbed his large, round, bald head. 'You mean you want to buy a side of beef?'

'Not at all, I wish to hire it and then return it within a very short space of time, any damage will be paid for upon its return.'

Abe closed one eye and looked at Daniel shrewdly with the other. 'What's you goin' to do with it?'

'Shoot it just the once.'

Henry's grin got even wider with delight. 'I told ya, didn't I? He's got some crazy plan.'

'Twenty dollars,' Abe snapped.

Henry's face went scarlet as he shook his finger at the butcher. 'Why, Abe Scantlebury, if you ain't the meanest man in this town . . . Don't you want to know why the marshal is goin' to shoot a side of beef?'

Abe folded his arms in defiance. 'Business is business.'

'Two dollars,' Henry said.

'Ten.'

'Two.'

'Eight.'

'Two.'

'Aw, come on, Henry. How about four?'

Henry shook his bald head. 'Two, and that's our final offer.'

Abe scratched his head in deep thought. 'What's you goin' to shoot it with?'

'A rifle,' Daniel replied.

The butcher's eyes suddenly grew wide with trepidation. 'What if that crazy Olga gets wind of it and shoots it with her scattergun?'

'I can assure you that will not be the case.'

Henry took out two dollars, grabbed Abe's hand and slapped them firmly in its palm. 'There,' he said. 'Now let's go and get the beef.'

The two men went into the rear of the store and came out with a side of beef between them. 'Where next?' Henry asked as the door opened.

'Ah, I see my deputy has arrived.' He turned to face Murphy. 'To the corral, I think. Follow me.'

As the four of them headed towards the corral, thirty or so of the townsfolk followed them, still lead by Stumpy. 'Hey, Henry,' he shouted again. 'Where you's goin' with that beef?'

'Over to the corral; the marshal's goin' to shoot it,' Henry replied.

'Either he don't know it's dead or he really hates beef!' Stumpy splurged as he took another drink.

When they arrived at the corral, the beef was placed in front of a bale of straw and Murphy pulled the trigger. Abe leaned over to Henry and whispered. 'What's he goin' to do next?'

138

'That's official business,' Henry replied.

In the excitement, Daniel hadn't noticed the gathering of townsfolk was getting bigger. 'There really is very little to see,' he tried to explain. 'All I am going to do next is reclaim the bullet from the straw bale.'

Joyous and spontaneous applause came from the spellbound crowd of forty whilst Abe and Henry took a bow. By this time Stumpy had run out of booze and energy, so he sat down and blew a raspberry at them both.

Daniel dug out the bullet carefully, quickly placed it in his pocket and turned to the absolute silence of a very disappointed crowd. 'Oh, very well,' he said as he departed whilst holding the bullet high in the air for all to see. The crowd went wild with delight.

Murphy returned to the jail but it wasn't long before Henry and Abe joined him. 'What are we goin' to next, Deputy?' Henry asked.

Murphy sat down and put his feet on the desk again. 'Wait for the marshal, I reckon.'

'What's with the shootin', Deputy?' Carver asked.

'That's just the marshal doin' what he does,' Murphy replied.

Suddenly the door burst open and Olga stood firm in the gap. She was carrying a large tin bucket and a brass ladle. 'I brings food for my man and zose I vish to kill,' she said.

The twins were right behind her carrying plates and a wicker basket covered in a blue and white gingham cloth. 'We have brought the food but there is a slight change of plan: the order has been changed,' Claude explained.

'Oh, yes, there has been a slight change, you might say,' Clarence added.

'I changes ze order and I come for to give zem beans. My big man has steak.' Without hesitation, Olga marched into the cells and began slopping beans onto the plates that the twins had only just managed to get into place. 'I prepares beans special, zey is wery goot.'

All five prisoners gave a false smile and accepted their fate as Olga finished dishing out their rations. 'I goes now. You eat.' As she passed Murphy she gave him a shy smile. 'I makes steak too,' she said.

The twins sat down to eat a selection of small triangular sandwiches as Murphy tucked his napkin under his chin and shook his head with delight. 'Boys, she's a mighty big woman and this is a mighty big steak,' he said.

After they had all finished, the twins gathered all the plates and stacked them ready for their return to Katie's Eating House, but before they could take them Daniel made his triumphant entrance. 'I see you stand like greyhounds in the slips, straining upon the start. The game's afoot: follow your spirit, and upon this charge, cry "God for Harry, England, and Saint George!"'

The twins almost burst with delight as they gave tumultuous applause. 'Bravo, bravo indeed,' they shouted.

Murphy looked on without emotion. 'Ain't nobody here called Harry nor George,' he drawled.

'And I ain't no saint.'

'Philistine,' he snapped, then, turning away to look at the twins, he said in a loud and clear voice. 'Gentlemen, I am happy to announce the bullet which killed Sheriff Hayes was fired by the very rifle we tested today, the rifle that belongs to Sheriff Stoppard.'

'That's a lie!' the sheriff shouted.

'I think not,' Daniel replied. 'There is no doubt your gun was used to kill the sheriff.'

'Someone must have taken it without me knowin',' Tom insisted.

Daniel walked slowly to the cells and looked Tom in the eyes. 'This is something for the courts to decide, but I have good reason to believe I will be able to collect more incriminating evidence in the near future; enough to see you convicted.'

Carver began to get agitated. 'I ain't done nothing, Marshal,' he protested. 'Bannister told me as how your deputy had been crowin' around town as he was faster than me, an' as I was yella all I did was to call him out and put a stop to his jawin'.'

'That true?' Murphy asked.

Carver crossed his heart. 'On my mother's grave,' he said with great sincerity.

'But I ain't never laid eyes on you afore.'

'Wait a second,' Daniel interrupted. 'Am I to assume you came to town with the full intention of engaging my deputy in a pistol competition?'

Carver dropped his jaw, shook his head and threw his arms out in total disbelief. 'And what's wrong with that, Marshal?'

'What is wrong? You were going to kill one another – and over some childish playground reputation?'

Carver pointed an accusing finger at Murphy. ''Taint my doin'. He was supposed to back down.'

'I ain't never backed down, not to no man, and I ain't never goin' to neither.'

Daniel gave his usual sigh. 'Once again, I bear witness to the most appalling torture of the English language. Somehow I feel the both of you must be related in some way. Possibly some common, rather distant ancestors came together for procreation purposes and were unfortunately successful, and through the annals of time you two are the result.'

Carver looked at Murphy. 'Does he always speak like that?'

Murphy nodded.

Daniel looked at the twins and pointed to the keys to the cells. 'Time to put an end to this comedy of errors: let this man out and deputise him immediately.'

'Let Carver out?' Murphy gasped.

'No, not Carver,' the marshal said sarcastically. 'Deputy Carver.'

CHAPTER 13

Soon after Carver was released from the cells, he retrieved his gun and placed it back into his holster with a smile. 'Sure do feel naked without it.'

Murphy looked nervously one way and the other as he took the marshal to one side in order to whisper in his ear. 'Are you out of your mind? Why have you made Carver a deputy?'

'From what I gather, he is a man of honour. His need to set things right after hearing of your false innuendos proves that his protestations about fair play not having taken place backs up my theory, and I feel he will be an asset rather than a hindrance. If you are still doubtful, there is an old expression that should satisfy your doubt, and it goes precisely like this: "keep your friends close and your enemies closer".'

'Are you saying he's my enemy still?'

'Not at all: I am merely trying to point out that if he were to be your enemy it would be a good idea to have him on our side.'

Murphy rubbed his chin, turned to Carver, beamed a smile and waved. 'Good to have ya with us, Carver.'

'I ain't never been no lawman before. There's somethin' strange about it; it makes my vest itch. I'm not sure I'm cut out for this sort of thing.'

'Oh, stuff and nonsense,' Claude jabbered. 'Mr Patterson took a while to get used to things and look at him now.'

'Indeed,' Clarence added. 'Now raise your right hand and place your left on this bible. Do you swear to uphold the law?'

Carver shuffled his feet nervously from side. 'I ain't certain – I ain't never done wrong by nobody but I ain't exactly done right neither.'

'Good gracious, man,' the marshal gasped. 'We are not looking for some sort of testimonial; all we are asking you to do is swear you will uphold the law.'

Carver looked up and pointed cautiously to the heavens. 'And somethin' else: I don't like to swear when you-know-who is listenin'; it don't seem right.' He took his hand off the bible and tilted his head. 'I don't wanna to go to tunk.'

'Tunk? Where on earth is tunk?' Daniel asked.

'Tunk, Marshal,' Murphy explained as he pointed a finger at the ground. 'It's where bad folk goes to.'

'That's right, Marshal, I don't like to swear when I've got His good book in my hand.'

'What on earth are you talking about, man? He

doesn't mean swear as in cursing, he means swear as one would do when taking an oath.' Daniel pointed to Clarence. 'Now ask him again.'

'Mr Carver, do you swear to uphold the law?'

'Oh dang my melt . . . I guess I dod gasted well do, and I'd like to say as to the past, well, I've done one or two bad things, things I ain't so proud of, but from now on I'm a changed man, Marshal. You can rely on that.'

Daniel stared at Carver. 'You know, I do believe you have less grey matter than a small pencil, so let me explain: the next time he asks you a question, any question, just say yes. Don't cough, sniff, or hesitate in the slightest – just say yes.'

Clarence replaced Carver's left hand on the bible and raised his right. 'Are you ready?' he asked.

'I sure am,' Carver replied.

'Do you swear to uphold the law?'

'I sure do.'

'That will have to do!' Daniel snapped. 'Otherwise we will be here until the four horsemen of the apocalypse appear.'

'Hell shit, Marshal. Four men and a couple of mules ain't no match for Carver and me. What do you say, Carver?'

'For sure, four riders from Acapulco ain't no match?'

Once again Daniel raised his eyes to the heavens. 'Well, gentlemen, whenever they do appear, you can rely on me to point them out.'

Both Murphy and Carver pushed their chests out

with pride. 'Thank you kindly, Marshal.' Carver said.

'Now, down to business,' Daniel began. 'Your first duty is to set free Ben and Tom Williams and escort them to the edge of town. Explain to them they must never return or their arrest will be of a more permanent nature.'

Claude began to bounce up and down in panic. 'Are you certain that is a wise move, Marshal?'

'Oh dear,' Clarence agreed. 'They are witnesses to murder after all.'

'Indeed they are,' the marshal explained. 'However, they are also witnesses to a great deal more, and that is why we must release them.'

Murphy stood and looked at Carver. 'Let's run them varmints out of town.'

'What do you want us to do, Marshal?' Abe asked.

'Hmmm? Go back to what you were doing before I asked for your help, I presume,' he replied offhandedly.

Henry and Abe looked dejected as they left the jail slowly. 'Well, I reckon as we'll be ready if you want us again, Marshal,' Henry murmured, but Daniel wasn't listening.

Murphy and Carver took the cell keys, let Tom and Ben out and marched them through the door at gunpoint. 'What about us, Marshal? Why aren't you letting us free? We ain't done nothing. What are we supposed to do?' Lucky Joe shouted as Daniel began to depart, leaving the twins in charge.

'Corruption wins not more than honesty. Still in

146

thy right hand carry gentle peace, to silence envious tongues,' he replied.

Joe looked at the sheriff. 'What in hell does he mean by that?' he said.

CHAPTER 14

The following day, Murphy and Carver patrolled the town, both wearing tin stars as proud as dogs with two tails. Wherever they went, townsfolk treated them with courtesy and respect, never failing to bid them good morning or doff their hats in recognition for a job well done. To both cowboys this was something new, something they loved, something worth striving for. Neither deputy said very much to one another; they just checked and nestled their pistols in their holsters constantly until they finally returned to the jail.

Inside, Murphy poured a coffee, gave it to Carver, got one himself, sat down behind the desk and lit a cigar. 'Sure does feel good,' he drawled.

Carver rolled himself a cigarette, carefully lit it, took a long draw and sat down next to the stove. 'Yep, it beats those long hot days on the trail and the even longer cold nights.'

'You know, Carver, it puzzles me: how come our paths ain't never crossed? I mean, I've been pushin' beef across four States and never run into you. . . .'

'Don't rightly know.'

'Then how come you're around these parts?'

'Came for work: times ain't what they were – the railway has seen to that. Times were beef was moved on the hoof – horses too, for that matter – but now things have changed.'

'I was a scout for the army once,' Murphy said. 'That was a ball-bustin' job if'n there ever were any.'

'The hell you say?'

'It sure was – I scouted for General Armstrong Custer himself. He was a sorry son of a bitch. Glad I got out before that puffed-up, ass-licking, yellow-haired polecat lost all those brave men at Little Big Horn.'

'Many a good soldier was lost there,' Carver agreed.

'I lost a wife because of that son of a bitch,' Murphy said solemnly.

'The hell you say?'

'Dancing Bird was her name – she sure was pretty. I'd gone and left her with her brother and sister to do some huntin'. I'd been gone a few hours when I saw smoke over the horizon. I knew somethin' was wrong so I galloped back real fast and found what those so-called soldiers had done.'

'The hell you say?'

Murphy nodded. 'I set her spirit free and left for good.' He took a drink of coffee and shook his head. 'Never went back – just got mean, I guess. Did a little bank robbin' and such like, until I got caught.'

'The hell you say?'

'Got five years, but me and the judge had a disagreement so that no-good varmint gave me twenty.'

'Twenty!'

'Twenty – that is, until those two twins gave me this job. All I got to do is keep the marshal alive for two years and all is forgiven.'

'Two years?' Carver gasped. 'How long to go?'

'More or less started,' Murphy explained.

Carver began to laugh. 'Murphy, that's one hell of a deal you got there.'

'Don't I knows it?' he grinned.

They remained in silence for a few minutes until Carver raised his head in thought. 'I had a wife once.'

'The hell you say?'

'Sure did. Lookin' back, we were just kids. I worked for her pa on his ranch; I worked real hard, too. We had been married for not more'n a few months when these riders came and burned down the ranch. Annabelle was killed. At first I did some drinkin', but one day I heard of a trail bum boastin' as to how he and five others run settlers off their land for the railroad so I found him and put a bullet in his leg. He was rollin' and screamin' on the floor, but he gave me the names of the others.'

'Did ya kill him?'

'No – I just left him there all helpless like, but it took me three years to track those murderin' bastards down.'

'I guess you shot 'em all?'

'I sure did – and every one was a fair fight, which was more'n they deserved.'

'I guess that's how you got your reputation as a gunslinger?'

'Sure is, and since then there's always someone who thinks they're faster, some young kid wantin' to make a name for himself, but the only name he gets is on a gravestone.'

'Marshal!' came Henry's voice from the street. 'Marshal!' he shouted as he ran breathless through the door. 'Bannister's here with around ten men.'

Murphy jumped up, grabbed a Winchester rifle, threw it to Carver and took the Remington. 'You certain it's Bannister?' he asked.

'Certain: he always wears that 'gator skin waistcoat and those brown leather britches. It's Bannister, all right,' Henry replied.

Carver looked through the window on the left. 'Where'd you seen 'em?'

'They is on the edge of town; we've got to warn the marshal.'

Murphy peered through the window on the right. 'I can't see nothing,' he said.

Henry mopped his brow as he sat down. 'They'll be headin' up the street in no time. What'll we do?'

Murphy looked hard at Henry. 'Can you shoot?' he asked.

'Well, I . . . I . . . I think so, well, not very good, but I have done a little shooting in my time.'

'Grab those guns over there. They belong to the sheriff and Joe but they ain't got no call to use 'em.'

151

'I can see 'em!' Carver said in excitement. 'Just comin' up the street, and there's old man Bannister himself right up front.' He gave a wry smile. 'I reckon I could pick him off from here.'

Murphy moved his position a little. 'I sees 'em. There must be ten or more.'

'What do ya reckon they want?' Carver asked.

'Those boys in there more'n likely.'

Bannister and his men lined up in front of the jail. 'Marshal!' Bannister shouted. 'There's no need for all of this to happen. Just give me the sheriff and Joe.'

'The marshal ain't here,' Murphy shouted. 'There's just Carver and me.'

Bannister dropped his head. 'Well, boys, that's too bad, 'cause in any case we'll take our boys by force if we have to, but I'm a reasonable man. If the both of you want to ride out of town and never look back, you have my word you'll be safe. I'll give you five minutes to think it over. Can't say fairer than that.'

Murphy and Carver thought deep and hard for most of the allotted time until Murphy broke the silence. 'I ain't never run away from a fight and I ain't goin' to start today, but Moses, if'n you want to go, that's fine by me.'

'You know, Murphy, I always knew my time would come from the barrel of a gun but I never knew when until now, so I ain't runnin' either.'

Murphy grinned like he'd never grinned before. 'How many do ya think we'll get before they gets us?'

'Can you shoot?' Carver asked.

'Better'n you.'

152

'Think so?'

'Know so.'

Carver held out his hand to shake a deal. 'Dollar a man, winner takes all?'

'Dollar an ear,' Murphy replied as he took Carver's hand.

'Bannister,' Murphy shouted. 'We're comin' out, but first you have to let the blacksmith go. He ain't part of it, you know that.'

Bannister stood tall, pulled up his pants and gave a triumphant smile. 'OK boys, send him out.'

As Henry got close to the door, he handed his guns over to them both. 'Good luck, boys,' he said. 'I ... I ... don't rightly know what to say other than that.'

'He's comin' out,' Murphy shouted as Henry opened the door and raised his hands.

'Don't shoot now, I ain't armed!'

'Now, what about you two deputies?'

Murphy and Carver flipped the safety loop off the hammers of their pistols and each shoved a second revolver in their belt. Slowly and deliberately, they went outside to face Bannister's men. Murphy pointed to Tom and Ben Williams. 'I see those two we let loose are with yer. We told 'em not to come back,' Murphy said. 'After we finish killin' you, they're next.'

'There are too many of us, boys, you don't stand a chance. Just drop those guns and ride away.'

'And the marshal?' Murphy asked. 'What'll you do with him?'

'That ain't your concern, boys. Ain't your concern.'

'We're makin' it our concern,' Carver said.

Bannister adjusted his gun-belt and shook his head. 'We have to get rid of him, you know that.'

'I suppose you'll back-shoot him like you did Sheriff Hayes.'

'I ain't never back-shot any man, but Sheriff Hayes had it comin'; he was poking about in business he had no right to.'

'So you had Tom Stoppard do your dirty work?'

'Gentlemen, if I may interrupt your farcical display, I beg to differ,' Daniel said from behind Bannister's men. 'Now, as marshal of this town, I am arresting you all. Therefore, if you would be so kind as to surrender all your weapons to my deputies, you will not suffer the consequences of resisting arrest. I do hope I make myself clear because for some reason, whenever I try to explain something in simple English, there often appears to be some sort of breakdown in communications.'

'That marshal of yorn must be plain loco,' Bannister said in disbelief.

'Oh dear, I was afraid you were going to be a little tiresome. Very well, this may explain things a little better.' The marshal was standing behind two large wooden barrels, and from one he produced an earthenware pot with a stout lanyard tied around its handle. One swing and the pot was on its way towards the gang, and Daniel dropped down securely behind both barrels. The pot smashed on landing and a hundred angry hornets swarmed out with the prime intention of stinging anyone they thought responsible for their plight.

All Bannister's men began to dance, swat, scream, roll and run as Murphy and Carver retreated safely inside the jail. Murphy looked out of the window. 'They sure do look mad,' he said with a grin. 'Looken those two tryin' to get into that god darn water trough.'

Suddenly, like the mighty Thor striking his anvil, Olga gave them a long range broadside from her scattergun, peppering Bannister's men with rock salt and much of the road and buildings around. As she was reloading, Bannister's men ran full tilt for their horses and rode away as quickly as they could, leaving only Bannister and his boys to do battle with the angry hornets. As the insect war began to wane, Murphy and Carver came back out and faced the gang of five.

'It's all over, Bannister,' Murphy said, cold as ice. 'Now drop them guns and put your hands high.'

Bannister had been stung and humiliated so his temper was up. He grabbed for his gun, but he was no match for Murphy and Carver as they both drew and fired in unison, one hitting Bannister in the forearm and the other his shoulder. 'Anyone else feel lucky?' Carver asked as he spat on the ground.

The other two could hardly see as they unbuckled their gun-belts, dropped them to the ground and raised their hands. 'This way, boys: just follow my voice,' Murphy said.

After they had been locked up safely, Murphy

joined Carver in the street and noticed a small gathering of townsfolk pointing to the wooden barrels. 'Where's the marshal?' he asked.

'Last I saw him, he was behind those barrels over yon'.'

Together they walked across the street, looked behind the barrels and found a large pile of blankets under which Daniel had taken cover. They lifted them and saw the marshal sitting squat with his fingers in his ears. 'Did we win?' he asked.

'Sure did, Marshal; that trick of yorn with those bees worked just fine. We've got Bannister and his boys locked up. The rest high-tailed it.'

Daniel brushed himself down before giving Murphy a withering look. 'For your information, they were not bees; they were hornets. Admittedly, both are from the same order, *Hymenoptera*, but quite different species nonetheless.'

Carver's eyes grew wide with excitement. 'Hey, I heard of that Hymen fella. Claimed he could get ya anythin' anyone wanted. Hymen Woolberg, if'n I'm not mistaken.'

'Well I'll be a son of a gun,' Murphy added with delight. 'Old Hymen used to bring us grits and victuals when I was knee-high to a grasshopper. How old will he be now?'

'Can't rightly say, but I once remember when we was on the range we met up with this travelling circus. Charlie Parker gave ten dollars to go and see and such because he thought there might be some ladies dancing about in their underwear. Anyway, there wasn't no such thing, but he done clapped eyes on this black-and-white-striped horse and wanted it something terrible. I can still remember when he came back all fired up and blabberin' about it as to how good one would look with his Sunday best an' all. Anyways, Old Hymen happened to be there and he told Charlie the horse he was wantin' was called a zebaree. I remembered the name good. Next thing, Hymen turns up with the zebaree and charged Charlie twenty-five dollars for it. I reckon the circus folk wanted to get rid of it real bad because it was a mean son of a bitch it was, always bitin' and kickin'. It wasn't no good for ridin' or pullin' a buggy and such, but it sure did taste good.'

'Whatever happened to Old Hymen?' Murphy asked.

'Him and his family moved east and opened a store, then another, then another until the name Woolbergs became real big.'

Daniel shook his head in disbelief.

CHAPTER 15

Later in the day, the marshal and the twins sat down in Katie's Eating House as Murphy and Carver stayed to guard the prisoners.

'Oh my,' Claude said with a smile. 'What a good day's work.'

'Yes, very good indeed,' Clarence agreed. 'And I am so glad we hired Mr Carver.'

'Indeed, my dear brother; he certainly proved to be an asset.'

'An asset indeed; so much so I think we need him to assist you with our next problem, Marshal.'

Daniel took a sip of tea. 'By what manner does this problem manifest itself?'

'It is a rather delicate matter, a matter that needs investigating in the most sensitive way possible.'

'Yes, indeed. Should the matter not be treated thus, a grave political situation could develop,' Claude pointed out.

'And to where are we going to travel?' the marshal asked.

'Not far: we will be staying at the Last Trading Post.'